English Magic

English *Magic*

USCHI GATWARD

GALLEY BEGGAR PRESS

First published in 2021
by Galley Beggar Press Limited
Norwich NR2 3LG

Text design and typesetting by Tetragon, London
Printed and bound by CPI Group (UK) Ltd, Croydon CR0 4YY

Of the stories in this collection:

'Backgammon' was first published in *The Dublin Review*, 2020

'What's for You Won't Go by You' was first published in *Yarn*,
a collaboration between Structo and Otherwhere, 2019

'Lurve' was first published in *gorse*, 2017

'Beltane' was first published by Galley Beggar Press, 2017

'Samhain' was first published in *Short Fiction*, 2016

'Oh Whistle and' was first published in *The White Review* online, 2016

'My Brother Is Back' was first published in *Wasafiri*, 2016

'On Margate Sands' was first published in *Flamingo Land &
Other Stories*, Flight Press (Spread the Word), 2015

'The Clinic' was first published in *Structo*, 2014

'The Bird' was first published in *Southword*, 2014

'The Crèche' (as 'Pink Lemonade') was first published in
the *Bristol Short Story Prize Anthology Vol. 6*, 2013

Paperback: 978-1-913111-10-6
Limited edition: 978-1-913111-09-0

For Pearl

CONTENTS

THE CLINIC

It's set up to look like a home, with sofas and a coffee table, but nobody's fooled. I haven't been here since she was a newborn. Stupid of me.

'She's a bit tired today,' I say. 'Busy day yesterday. We went to the park. She didn't want to get up this morning.'

The clinician smiles briefly, a little wanly. Her assistant sets out cubes on a mat on the floor. At the touch of a keypad a mounted camera in the corner swivels towards us. Behind a glass screen another clinician watches.

Cara's spotlessly dressed in her smartest clothes. I'm wearing my dumbest outfit, complete with slogan.

Dean clears his throat. 'She might not be at her best,' he says.

'Put her down on the mat,' says the clinician.

I put Cara down and she reaches immediately for the shapes. She looks at them. Starts to put them together, clumsily. She piles them up but they fall down.

'This is normal,' says the assistant. 'By eighteen months she'll be able to do it.'

'Does she babble?' says the clinician.

'Babble?' says Dean. 'Oh yes – she talks.'

She sure as hell didn't get her brains from him.

'Talks?'

'Gabber-gabber-gabber,' says Dean. 'Mum-mum-mum.'

The assistant smiles.

'Is she walking yet?' says the clinician.

I shake my head. 'She crawls a lot more than this normally,' I say, as the assistant holds out a toy to her, arm's length away. 'She's a bit tired from yesterday is all.'

Cara crawls towards the toy. The clinician seems satisfied and touches the screen on her device. 'We don't record brain activity this time,' she says. 'Just run basic checks.'

She taps her keypad and a Perspex box to our right emits a high-frequency sound. Cara turns towards it and a puppet waves at her. She laughs. The clinician repeats the task several times, different frequencies and different directions. Then with no sound, just the puppets waving.

The assistant passes Cara a pen. Cara pincers her fingers. 'Good.' Into her device she says: 'T33. NA.'

'We'll see you again at fifteen months,' says the clinician. She consults her screen. 'Which will be some time in June.'

Cara stares at my T-shirt and starts to form a shape with her mouth. I scrunch up the shirt and zip up my jacket.

Back in the anteroom she's weighed and measured, her stats plotted on a graph – reassuringly unexceptional for her age – and then we are free to go.

We walk home. From her buggy Cara says, 'I liked the puppets.' And then she falls asleep.

We take the path by the nature reserve. The daffodils are out.

'We got away with it,' says Dean. 'For how much longer, though?'

At home, I put Cara to bed to sleep off the cough syrup. Over dinner I say, 'I wonder if we just don't talk in front of her.'

'We can't keep her with us for ever,' he says.

★

At Wednesday baby group she's spotted. By one of the other mums, newish. Her child's well dressed. New spring trousers already, rolled up at the cuff. Woollen waistcoat and brown leather boots, though he's hardly walking. One of those.

Cara's sitting in the toy kitchen, stirring some play food round and round in a pan.

'She's a clever little thing, isn't she?' Harsh-eyed.

I laugh. 'Is she? Saves it all up for when we go out then.'

'What you got there, Cara?' says the woman.

'Egg,' says Cara.

The woman purses her mouth and says nothing more, eyes hard with satisfaction. Cara abandons her saucepan and crawls to the bookcase, clambering up it and pulling down picture books much too old for her. I read them to her to quieten her down but I know that the woman can see me, peering over from her place at the sand table.

After the session the manager catches me. She wants to make a film of me reading to Cara. She's never seen a baby that likes books so much. I laugh uneasily.

'Think about it,' she says.

★

I stop taking her to the groups so regularly. I tell people she's had a cold. I tell them we're going to the park more often now that the weather's better.

'I hope she'll be walking by summer,' I say. 'I can't wait.'

And I get people to give me tips about trikes and trousers and surfaces to try her on. I go to the more active groups, leave the quieter ones alone. But a week or two later I lift Cara onto the top of a slide and she says, 'One, two, three – go!' quietly, but I look around and there's the new woman, watching me.

'Go!' I say, and push Cara down the slide.

I look up again and she's still looking. She holds my gaze for a moment and then slowly turns away.

At lunch that day, Cara counts out her beans onto her high-chair, one to twenty.

'If I eat one, it will be nineteen,' she says.

'That's right,' I say.

'If I eat two, it will be eighteen.'

I don't reply.

'Mummy? It will be eighteen.'

'Eat your beans,' I say.

After lunch she wants me to read to her. I say no – no more books now, I'm tired. While I load the dishwasher she crawls to the pile and pulls one out, then sits on the floor and studies it, turning the pages delicately. She furrows her brow. I take it from her, gently, and switch on the TV.

★

I'd heard of this before, on the internet. Archived chats. Coded suggestions. Always accompanied by post deletions. And then posters who just stop posting. It doesn't end well.

I start to overbuy, little by little, in my grocery order – small, cheap things that won't be noticed by the software; things that are easy to pack and that don't require cooking. Flat tins of sardines are the best, but I have to be careful – too many will raise a flag, so I get one extra every week – just enough to look like the baby's eating more and likes tinned fish, I reckon. I vary the other items – one week hot dogs, another baked beans. In this way I collect twelve tins within six weeks.

We eat a bit less, and save what else we can. We run through everything in the store cupboard – anything we can't take – and eat that instead. Pasta, rice, noodles, dried pulses, instead of valuable tins and vacuum packs.

I go to a shop in the next district and spend some of next month's tokens there, filling my basket with party foods and a small birthday cake. I buy birthday candles too, and a birthday banner, and household candles, and a cigarette lighter. In another shop on the way home I buy another lighter.

At baby group, I sow the seeds. I give out that we'll be staying with my sister for the summer, with a view to moving there. I tell them she's got an allotment.

'It won't feed all of you, though,' says the new woman, sharply.

'Maybe not, but we're going to learn how to work on it,' I say, mildly. 'My sister doesn't have the energy to make the most of it, she's not in good health. And we'll pool our tokens. Anyway, it's not definite – we'll see how we get along over the summer and then think about it.' I smile.

'I didn't know you had a sister,' says one.

'No... we haven't seen much of each other in recent years. She's not in good health.'

'What about Dean's job?' says someone else.

I sigh. 'That's part of it really. We always worry about him being laid off, things never look good. He can pick up some work with my brother-in-law over the summer, and then his boss'll take him back on afterwards if it doesn't work out. We won't need much money out there. They've got a generator.'

I wish I had a sister. With an allotment and a generator.

13

Some safe place where Cara could be well, and we'd just be country bumpkins, not worthy of notice. The clinic appointment comes through, and I open it with a lurch.

Cara needs a pox jab. She's not quite old enough for it, but we'll have to be gone before she is. I could take her and tell them that we know someone who's got it, but we might be caught out, and we can't risk that. I could go to the walk-in centre in a panic and say I saw a boy with spots, and act a bit stupid when they ask for details, but it's still a risk. But then we'll come up on the records anyway when we miss the jab in half a year's time.

I take the risk, at the walk-in centre, and they agree to do her. Cara knows what's up. When she sees the needle she screams. 'No, Mummy! Hurts!' The nurse doesn't bat an eyelid. I realize that she hasn't looked at Cara's date of birth.

*

On Dean's day off I leave him with Cara and head out to pick up the last supplies. The camping shop is in the next district but one, in a row of specialist traders. I've passed it before but never had any call to go in. As I push the door, a bell ting-tings. Proper old school. A skinny old man comes out of the back of the shop, newspaper in hand, and nods 'Morning' to me before taking a seat on a stool behind the counter and settling back down to read. I take out my phone and scroll down my list, brushing through the racks of cagoules, examining elasticated inner cuffs and breathable linings. I look at map protectors and whistles and torches, and then at thermal underwear.

'Looking for anything in particular?' says the man, eyes still fixed on his newspaper.

'I've got a list,' I say, going over to him.

He looks at it, then up at me. 'Where you going?'

'Spending the summer at my sister's in Suffolk.'

'And you'll need a tent there, will you?'

'We might do some camping while we're there. Explore the countryside.'

'Might you. Nothing firmly planned then?'

'I'll see what the prices are.' I shrug and move away. 'We'll need the clothes anyway, got nothing suitable.'

I wander over to the small bookshelf and run my hands idly over the spines. Birdwatching... wildlife... birdwatching... birdwatching for children... angling... geology. I pick up a second-hand paperback, *Foraging*, and flip through the pages, stopping to read. I sense him watching me and snap it shut. It puffs up a cloud of dust.

'When I was younger a lot of people used to do it.' He smiles and looks at me intently.

The bell ting-tings and a middle-aged man comes in, asking for waterproof trousers in a Large. He buys them and leaves.

The owner watches me for a while as I try out binoculars, then eases himself up off his stool and beckons me to follow, round the L of the shop, through an archway.

In the inner room recess, three mannequins dressed head to toe in waterproofs – a man, a woman, and a child a little older than Cara, her dark hair cut into a bob with a blunt fringe – crouch round a campfire, in attitudes of rigor mortis. The mother, skin a waxy yellow, eyes full and staring, whistle dangling from a lanyard round her neck, clutches the cup from a thermal flask. Three silver sleeping bags – one junior-sized – sit neatly rolled in the pop-up tent behind them. Kendal mint cake and firelighters litter the groundsheet. A square of tinfoil lines the portable grill.

I inspect the tent, shiny green nylon, just big enough for one person, or one person and a child. 'I'll take the lot,' I say, turning to him.

'Sizes?' he says, going to his stockroom, and I tell him, giving Cara's next size up.

He piles the bagged-up clothes and boxed-up boots and gear on the counter, then comes out from behind it with a packet in his open palm.

'Sterilizing tablets, in case you can't boil your water.' He shows me and chucks them on the pile.

He pulls things off the shelves and out of drawers. 'A flask – when you do boil water, put some in a flask. Then you have it even when your fire's gone out.

'Medical kit – essential.

'Thick winter gloves – also good for picking nettles. You can eat nettles, you know. Yes – once you cook them they don't sting. That's where your flask of hot water comes in handy.' His thin mouth stretches over his teeth in a smile. 'They also make good tea, for when you've drunk all the real stuff.'

Has he been questioned before, I wonder, about branded goods on people found (alive?) in the woods, in caves? I'd love to ask him whether they were found alive. I wonder if he ever hears back from anyone. How he knows what works.

'Do you sell anything else?' I ask, looking at him directly. He looks away. And then goes to the door of his back room. I wonder if it's an invitation to follow.

I make another circuit of the shop. I choose a large waterproof camper bag, maps, torches, penknives and binoculars. I pick up the *Foraging* book and *Birdwatching for Children*.

'Oh, and I might take these,' I say carelessly, dropping them onto the counter. Then I hand over the equivalent of three weeks' pay.

As he packs up my purchases into the camper bag, he passes me a card. 'Do come back,' he says. 'We do mail order too.' And he smiles again, revealing a false crown.

★

At home I pack the dried foodstuffs into the camper bag – cheesy biscuits, packets of small cakes, raisins and chocolate – and all the tins. Candles. Cutlery. Vitamins. Toiletries. Jewellery. Cash. Nothing electronic. A few warm clothes, mostly things for Cara. Wellies in two child sizes. We'll wear the rest. Dean collects up all his lighters from when he used to smoke, before the pollution got too bad. I used to tease him for being a hoarder. I stuff in a couple of print books for Cara. We eat the birthday cake.

Late at night, in the kitchen, with the washer on, I read about foraging, committing to memory the properties and seasons of fungi, berries, leaves, bulbs, roots, flowers, nuts and seeds. I make Dean learn about them too, in case we get split up. One day I'll teach Cara, if we last that long.

I redraw the maps on paper, using code words for the names of places and marking in South as North. I make copies for both of us. We've got an old compass that belonged to Dean's granddad. I don't know how to use it but I'll figure it out. I know how to use the sun.

It's hard to leave all of Cara's baby things, but if we hang on to the past we lose the future. Nothing to keep them for anyway: no chance of having another one now. I don't want anyone else to have them, so I burn them in a metal waste bin on the balcony, one box at a time, one Sunday afternoon.

I tell our neighbours on both sides and down the walkway that we'll be gone for the summer. Dean tells his boss that we might not be back.

We're lucky the weather's still cool when we leave in June. No one will comment on our anoraks. We dress as holidaymakers, in light hiking gear, Dean in shorts.

At our local shop I use some more of next month's tokens for picnic food. Some of it will keep for another day – and the tokens are no good to us now. I tell the shopkeeper we're away for the summer. He knows us. 'Sister's got an allotment!' I say. And 'Dean's got a holiday job!'

The last thing I do is tell the clinic we'll be on holiday when the check is due – gone for the whole summer. No, we don't have time to reschedule: we're leaving today. The receptionist huffs with frustration, especially when I say I don't know exactly when we'll be back.

'She's hitting all her milestones...' I say.

'That's not the point!' she snaps, and huffs a bit more as she types something. 'Just call for an appointment as soon as you're home,' she says. 'I'll make a note to contact you in September, just in case.'

My heart gives a little leap.

I know that if they want to find us they will. I just have to hope that they don't care enough. We're nothing valuable to them – at least, they don't know that we are.

*

When we get to the forest, we look for an area with good cover, not too far from a stream. We find a small place surrounded by bushes. We can stay here for a while, and maybe come back here too. Some of the bushes are evergreens, so they'll shield us in the winter. I mark the place on our maps. We use branches and a picnic blanket, and cover them with ferns to build a bivouac. I set out bowls to catch rainwater. We take off our layers of clothes and pack them away, back in the waterproof bag. We make a light camp; we might need to move quickly.

We build our first fire, just for the practice: dry leaves and twigs, one match, one candle, smiling in the glow of it. We eat sardines and madeleines. I read Cara her book and brush her nine teeth. While she sleeps in the tent, I leave the camp and scrape the dirty nappies with leaves, then wash them in the stream. When I get back I curl against her. A fine rain patters on the bivouac, but in our sleeping bags we are warm, and it will only get warmer this summer. We should be hardened enough when October comes round.

In the morning I wash myself, upstream of the nappies. I find some field mushrooms on the banks, and cut them with my penknife: they smell fresh and mouldy, damp with dew or rain. I walk back jubilant, a longer way, so as not to make a path between our camp and the stream. Nettles grow everywhere. I'll pick some later, to stew with the mushrooms.

As I cross a clearing, a huge auburn fox, the biggest I've seen, as big as a pig, pounds past me, a hare in its jaws. Another, younger fox chases it. I watch them hurtle through the wet trees, flashing tawny and white.

When I return to the camp, Cara is standing outside. She is barefoot. She fixes me with her eyes and takes two tiny steps on the forest floor, then a pause, then one more. I run to her and scoop her up, then show her the mushrooms, which she wants to eat immediately. I wipe them on a cloth, slice them and put them in the pan.

'Dean, I'm going back for nettles,' I shout, and I grab my winter gloves.

I wonder about the foxes, and the other things. Will we be their prey, when the weather turns, when the ice sets in?

I wonder about loneliness.

Maybe we'll find some of the others? There must be others.

MY BROTHER IS BACK

He was woken one evening and told that he was going home.

They drove in silence – a slow, heavy, quiet car with tinted windows. He wore handcuffs tethered to leg shackles, but no goggles this time. The two agents held his upper arms on the way to the car, and sat in the back seat with him.

It was dark outside and the windows were dark. The car moved through the wide and low-lit streets of the town, the sidewalks empty and frosted, and he felt more than saw the movement as they turned the corners, soft headlamps lighting the way. It was like one of those games he played as a child, where the victim was blindfolded and turned around and around and around and led somewhere. And then they were on a motorway – a freeway – and they fell into a line with other cars.

He did not seriously believe they were taking him to the airport until they arrived at the bright lights and glass of the terminal entrance. But then they drove past the building and on, out onto the tarmac. They got out and the car disappeared, swinging silently round and moving off.

There were steps leading up to a hole in the jetbridge, and he shuffled up these, escorted by the agents and security, the pilots and cabin crew watching. A lipstick-smiling blonde greeted him at the threshold: 'Hello, how are you, welcome aboard.'

Once on the plane, his restraints were removed. The trapdoor was closed and the steps wheeled away. A few minutes later, the other passengers boarded.

The first ones he saw were an Uncle and Auntie type, grey beard, hijab and saree. It seemed a good omen. The woman glanced at him across the empty cabin, and briefly smiled.

When they left the East Coast behind, he looked across the aisle to see glimpses of the land receding. He had once wanted to see the United States. But this was the last he would set eyes on them now.

The agents spoke to each other occasionally on the flight. One read a book – some light fiction by an American author. The other did nothing except stare ahead with eyes open, except when wanting to eat or drink or use the toilet, and then the novel-reader would put down his book and pay attention.

The American stewardess looked at him and at the men on either side as she handed him down his halal meal. It was better than prison food.

He watched the progress of the plane. He had once appreciated the limbo of airports and journeys; after eight years, though, limbo was losing its appeal. He would have liked to have watched a film, but he did not want to with the agents watching him. When he needed the toilet, one of them accompanied him and waited outside the door. He went several times, for the chance to walk through the plane, and to look at his face in the unbreakable mirror. Some of the passengers glanced up as the bearded Asian and the tall white man passed by, repeatedly, always in tandem.

Back in his seat, he looked across to the windows to see the sky. At one point the Auntie went past and seemed about to speak to him, a smile playing on her lips, but changed her mind. After a few hours of it he fell asleep.

★

Now at Heathrow, the agents take him through security and immigration, flashing their badges.

And then they leave him. Once they're through passport control they stop, and the novel-reading one holds out his passport and says, looking over the top of his head rather than at his face, 'OK. You're free to go.' And then they leave.

Trolleys and suitcases wheel past him on the polished floor, which bounces light. He holds his passport.

Airport security is everywhere. The eyes of uniformed men run over him and rest on him. He has no money but he dare not beg for change.

He wonders if they know who he is, if they've been alerted, and then decides that they don't – they are suspicious of him anyway. And he is not big news any more.

'Ringing for you now.' The reverse-charge call goes through to his parents' house.

He senses the presence of the operator on the line. Calls to his brother and parents from prison, always with a rasping, rushing sound in the background, and a clicking occasionally.

'There's no answer from that number, caller.'

'I'd like to try another one.'

He gives his brother's flat, and then his parents' shop: the only landlines he has dialled in eight years. There is no answer from these either. Putting a call through to a mobile is not allowed. He guesses at the number of an aunt.

Uncle Greybeard and Auntie Hijab emerge from passport control. He considers approaching them, but decides not to risk it. The Auntie smiled so nicely at him before; he'd prefer not to see the shutters slam down.

'There's no dial tone, sir. Are you sure you have the correct number?' Slightly testily.

What does it matter to you? he thinks. Are you on commission? But there is nothing else he can dredge up and so he rings off and hangs up the phone.

Outside the airport he finds the taxi rank. His tracksuit top is tight around his shoulders now, and somewhat too thin. From across the concourse he suddenly sees the agents, watching him in plain view from behind the glass of the terminal.

When he reaches the front of the queue, the driver's eyes flick up and down over him, taking in his lack of luggage but saying nothing.

He gives his parents' address in the suburbs to the south and east of Heathrow.

'Seventy quid alright?' says the driver, after a pause.

It sounds too much but he is not in a strong bargaining position. He looks across at the agents and around at the queue massed behind him.

'Alright,' he says.

He gets in the back. He closes his eyes and shields his forehead with a hand, to indicate he does not wish to be disturbed. The driver drives.

After a safe distance he removes his hand from his eyes and looks around, still careful to give no encouragement to conversation.

He wonders if he is being followed. A blue Toyota tails them for some time, leaving the motorway with them at Junction 10, then to his relief takes the exit for Cobham. But there would not be just one car, unless the objective was simply to spook him rather than track him effectively. The driver of a white Lexus now seems to be taking an unhealthy interest in the cab.

He laughs out loud at his initial thought back in the airport, that they really had been letting him go. That he was free.

He catches the cabbie's eye in the mirror, but they do not speak. How green it is here, even with the trees bare, even on the edge of the city. Fields and parkland. So much grass.

They pass Morden Hall and he sees the mosque. From here he could easily walk it. He looks out at the road on either side, at the changes in buildings and signage.

At Eastfields the cab leaves the main road and cuts through side streets. They seem to have shaken off the Lexus.

They approach his parents' road and he directs the cabbie to the house. There is no car in the driveway.

'My parents will pay the fare,' he says. 'Wait here.' And he gets out before the cabbie can respond.

Gravel crunches under his feet. There are new rose bushes in the front garden, a few dried petals clinging on, and heavy planters bearing evergreen shrubs on either side of the front door.

He rings the bell. He can make out a light further down the hallway. He rings again, then looks back at the cabbie, whose face registers mild annoyance. No sign of them in the front room, though he notes that they have a new television and curtains.

He rings once more then walks back to the cab.

'I'm sorry, they must be at their shop. It's only a few streets away.'

As the cab turns into the road he can see that the shop is shut. He gets out anyway and tries the door handle, peers through the glass, playing for time. He presses the buzzer once, twice, holding down his finger.

There's no answer. The driver is watching him from the cab. He is trying to think of other local addresses when the tenant in the flat above the shop throws up the dirty sash and leans out into the street, filling the frame of the window. He is wearing white Panjabi pajama.

He steps back off the kerb and shouts up to the tenant, 'I'm Mr Ahsan's son.'

'Syed?' The man's eyes widen. 'Wait.'

He hears running down the stairs. The man opens the door, lets him in ('Go upstairs. Go') then goes out into the street and pays the cab.

Syed leaves his shoes at the top of the stairwell and enters the flat. He has not been in it since he was a child. A patchy carpet of worn rugs covers the floor, the lino cold against his stockinged feet, and two 1950s armchairs with wooden legs are set at angles to each other in the room. A half-wall of kitchen units divides the space into two rooms. He suddenly remembers being a small boy sleeping in the big bed the other side of the partition, while his mother cooked in the kitchenette, huge pans on a little stove. He remembers that there is a shower and toilet leading off the bedroom, and being washed by his mother in a plastic tub in the shower stall.

He hears the street door shut and the latch click, and the cab drive off, and the tenant comes up the stairs again.

The tenant kicks off his chappals and picks up the enamelled coffee pot on the stove, waving it aloft. 'Do you want coffee? Would you prefer tea?'

Syed nods.

The tenant pauses for a moment, and then spoons coffee grounds into the pot. He rubs his hands. 'It's a bit cold in here, eh? Are you cold? Here, have a blanket. I can put the heating on.'

25

'No... thank you.'

'Have you eaten?'

'Not since the plane.'

'I can heat you some soup.' He holds up a can in big hands. 'Heinz Cream of Tomato.'

Syed nods. Holding the folded blanket to his chest, he watches the tenant rip the lid off the can, empty the contents into a tiny milk pan and fire up another gas ring.

The tenant lays a spoon and a plate of bread on a Formica card table patterned in the middle with scratches. He stirs the soup. The coffee pot bubbles and he pours black liquid into two toughened-glass cups.

Syed stirs in sugar and milk. He takes a sip and then warms his hands on the cup. His teeth begin to chatter. He arranges the blanket around his shoulders and back. The man takes the pan off the hob and scrapes the soup into a bowl.

The bowl is chipped. Syed looks up. 'My parents will pay you back the money as soon as they come.'

The tenant waves a hand. He watches Syed eat. 'I can get more food if you want it. I have the key to the shop.'

Syed shakes his head. 'Why's the shop shut?'

'It's Friday, man.' He laughs. 'I'm not a very good Muslim.' He smiles at Syed. 'Do your parents know you're coming? They never said.'

'I didn't know myself until last night. I tried to call them from the airport.'

The tenant picks up his mobile and dials. He shakes his head. 'Phone's switched off. Still in the mosque, or visiting someone.' He turns on the lamp and goes for the curtains.

'Could you leave them?' says Syed. 'I'd like to see outside.'

'Of course. Yes. Of course.'

Syed finishes his soup. The tenant clears it away and sits back down opposite him.

He leans forward. 'I've followed your case,' he says. 'In the papers. Al Jazeera. Sometimes the BBC.'

Syed nods.

The tenant nods. 'Eight years,' he says.

Syed passes a hand over his eyes.

'Would you like to sleep?'

'I am very tired.'

The tenant drags out a small couch. 'Here.' He puts two cushions at the head.

Syed rises from his chair and moves heavily to the couch. Now that the lamp is on, the darkness seems to fall faster around it, this pool of yellow light the only lit space in the world. He lies down and the tenant draws the blanket over him.

'Shall I leave the curtains open? The light on?'

'Yes. Please.'

'Should I try your parents again?'

Syed shakes his head and closes his eyes. 'It's OK,' he says. 'I can wait.'

OH WHISTLE AND

God has very particular political opinions.

JOHN LE CARRÉ

M is whizzing round the Cheltenham Waitrose, throwing sugar snap peas, prawns, rice noodles, ready-sliced peppers and pumpkin soup into her half-sized trolley. Oh, and milk.

L is setting out the exercise books and children's drawings ready for parents' information evening.

Z swaps his Oyster cards in his wallet before leaving the house, switching to his other, pre-reg card for the journey from home to the party meeting. It means he misses out on the daily cap but hey.

Y has never registered her Oyster card – even though it makes claiming back her work receipts a PITA – because she doesn't trust the government. It's a total waste of time, because the government can already track her via her smartphone, but she doesn't realize that. (The other reason it's a waste of time is that she's not as interesting as she thinks she is.)

J, who trusts the government even less, doesn't have an Oyster card. He pays through the nose for his privacy, and he can't use the buses. Mostly he cycles. In the new year the cash option is being taken away from the Underground, so he won't be able to use that either. Ah well – it's not like he has to be anywhere.

Z leaves his main phone at home and takes the second handset, with the battery and SIM card removed and taped to the housing. He pulls up his hood.

On her way to the tills M passes a young man still wearing his green lanyard over his sweater. She nods at it and he takes it off, stuffing it into his bag.

L goes through her bank statement while she's waiting, and thinks about cancelling her union subs – there is less pressure to belong these days, and she has never made use of them, can't see any reason why she would. She just has to get around to telling payroll, because she pays by automatic check-off.

Z also pays by automatic check-off. He has no problem with his employers knowing he is a member of the union. Indeed, it would be rather dim-witted of them not to notice.

At M's workplace it's mandatory to disclose union membership. And after all, it's not like they couldn't find out, ha ha.

The first parents arrive and L welcomes them.

At the meeting Z runs into H, whom he hasn't seen all summer. Busy, she says. But less busy now. They sit together.

M's tennis coach asks what she does for a living. Oh god, boring desk-monkey stuff, she says. I wish I had a talent, like you.

At L's information evening one of the mothers asks for more books featuring non-whites. Well, what she actually says is, Hey – 1978 called. It wants its reading scheme back. And: These are so white they make my eyes hurt.

Her words, and the views they express, tick a couple of the boxes on L's PREVENT checklist. This is a relief, because it means that at last L can fill out a profile form and lodge it with SLT, who will pass it to CHANNEL and perhaps to AVERT.

Which means that she's being vigilant, that she's on-task, that she's keen, she's aligned (being aligned is one of the conditions for performance-related pay).

And: If the parents have nothing to hide then they've nothing to fear. That was one of the mantras from the training course.

V, who is the parent in L's sights (and shortly to be in the sights of the SLT and CHANNEL and possibly even AVERT), has a wide circle of acquaintance (another thing that makes L nervous, though she hasn't articulated that to herself).

V doesn't wear a headscarf, but then she's a more modern, jeans-wearing type. In the training L and her colleagues were told that traditional dress wasn't necessarily a marker. It *could* be, the trainer clarified, but not necessarily.

L completes her report, seals it in an envelope and puts it in the SLT pigeonhole.

★

In the last week O has looked at various maps of Xi'an, read up on the political history of Shaanxi province, compared kettles on the Argos site, watched *Panorama* on catch-up and listened to an old Chomsky lecture. Right at this moment, O is browsing the Snowden archive and downloading a pamphlet by the erstwhile Muslim Council of Britain (which later this morning will catch the attention of M).

(Funnily enough the associate editor of *The Spectator* registers an identical browsing history – apart from the kettles – but, notwithstanding he is inconvenient, no one thinks he is a terrorist.)

In Bucharest, C, working for the Ministry, reads up on the work of M's department.

In Phoenix, Arizona, a server records that one of its hosted sites has been accessed by O.

In Xi'an, the Muslim communities organize, via careful use of WeChat.

Classy as ever, NewsGlobal has moved on from hacking the handsets of dead children, and is now hacking the teenaged offspring of the Labour leader.

★

L catches V at pick-up time.

Why should I complete it? says V. Tell me why.

So that we have it on record, says L. Your refusal.

V is shaking the sheaf of papers. It shows contempt, she says – *contempt* – for a huge swathe of the population. I can't believe you can't see that.

Look, we don't make the vaccine, says L. We don't even write the forms. We just distribute them. And we just need you to sign them.

And you can't see the message it sends? says V. Hindus, Muslims, Jews, you can all fuck off.

Well it doesn't quite say that, says L.

V shakes her head at L. You just don't get it, do you? This is what started the Indian Mutiny, she says. At L's blank look she throws her hands up at the ceiling and then shakes them at L: Look it up.

Z's workplace union is trying a different tack. Management seems to have got wind of a few things lately that could only have been got from the union minutes. The workplace rep, W, who suspects hacking on the part of the management, has set a bear trap, seeding the minutes with fictitious nonsense. Sure enough, the fictitious nonsense appears on the SMT agenda. (How does W know this? Because the union is hacking the management, and has been for quite some time.)

Z is tasked with writing up the minutes by hand, photocopying them privately away from the workplace, and distributing them personally to each member, just before 5 p.m.

On the train home L reads the flu vaccine form properly. It just says that yes, it contains porcine gelatine, and yes we still recommend you allow your child to have it even if you are from a religion that doesn't eat pork, and no, there isn't a pork-free alternative available.

OK, she can see that it's a problem, yes. All sorts of people have dietary issues – and why aren't they developing a pork-free alternative? On the other hand, it's not like anyone is allergic to pork. (Are they?) Not like nuts.

And in this world, we all need to make compromises. L makes them every day. And she does it without calling anyone a racist.

By the time L reaches Whyteleafe South she's decided it's something else for PREVENT.

Yes. V is *clearly* engaged in an ideology. OK, maybe not. But she's being deliberately obstructive, isn't she? Which shows, doesn't it, that she's developed Them and Us thinking? She might even have attitudes that justify offending – not to say that *she* would necessarily justify offending, but her attitudes might. Mm, yes. (L was raised a Catholic, and can be Jesuitical when she wants to be.) All of this requires a report.

M's tennis coach is working his way up to asking her out. She thinks through the logistics of this one.

Fuck! L has looked up the Indian Mutiny. This is scary stuff. In the light of what L's just read, V's words are practically a threat.

★

33

The management is getting twitchy about the lack of union minutes. Normally they are done within a day or two of the meeting, on company time.

And then, as soon as they are circulated, management relaxes visibly. The intercept is obviously still working. But how?

W, the union leader, now suspects a management mole – probably one of the recent recruits. She calls a secret, off-site meeting of her lieutenants, who include Z. She is going to set another bear trap.

Going through the completed vaccine forms, which are *finally* all back, except V's, of course (L really, *really* wishes the parents could do things without needing to be reminded), L notes that two of the other families have refused permission. One child has an allergy and one is a Muslim. She'll refer the Muslim refusal under PREVENT – makes sense, if she's referring V. Just so it's clear she's not singling her out. There are two other Muslims in the class whose parents have agreed to the vaccine. In one case L knows it's because the mum can't read English, but then that's her lookout. Get a translator! No way would L sign a form she hadn't read.

Come to think of it, this flu vaccine is a really useful tool for PREVENT. L wonders if the other class teachers are being as vigilant. Perhaps she should drop an email to SLT.

Z is to handwrite two sets of minutes – one with red herrings and one with different red herrings – and distribute Herrings A to those three people whom Z, W and P have identified as potential moles. Herrings B are to go to everyone else.

It is a risky strategy, P says.

W agrees, but what other option do they have, short of actual menace? The likelihood of people comparing documents is very small, she says, because they think they all have the same. Everyone has been told not to bring the minutes into work – they are handed them personally as they leave the site, and told not to bring them in again. This has been reiterated many times. Anyway, if they do rumble us, all they'll know is that we're on to them.

Which will make them more careful, says P.

In Cheltenham, the analysts have made a connection between Z and O. At 1.35 p.m. Z added the editor of the *New Humanist* on Facebook. Though innocuous enough, this brings him within a pattern of contacts that mirrors that of the Leeds group, and of O.

There is nothing else in the metadata to link them. There is nothing yet to warrant a content search. But if a link goes live, there will be.

Z has been sure all along that the government has him in its sights. And now, for the first time, he is right.

Z and O do not know each other, and have never been in contact, but they do have some common interests, which tend towards the political. Neither of them is in contact with the Leeds group, but again, there is metadata tracking a potential link, which, if activated (a friend request, a Twitter follow), trips the trap.

★

Management have got the first herrings and not the second ones (unless, of course, it's a double bluff). This means that the potential moles are, as suspected, one or more of S, Q and E. Now to narrow it down.

M's colleague R analyses a pattern of communications traffic around the Notts–Derby area, which shows some parallels with Leeds (although no contact). R presents her findings briefly, at the team meeting.

W, Z and P watch S, Q and E, through glass-walled meeting rooms, at their desks, on their way to lunch. They switch rabbits every couple of hours so as not to attract suspicion. On a smoke break, P tells Q that W is plotting something big with the rep on the Essex site. Keep it under your hat.

M sits in the canteen with a baked potato and a killer Sudoku, wondering what to do about the tennis coach.

Sure enough, Q can't wait to spill the beans. After lunch Z sees her slip into the glass-walled office of A and sit down. A's face is too interested to be listening to a variation in the monthly stats.

M decides to dodge the question entirely by letting her tennis lessons lapse for a while. It's too cold for tennis anyway – time enough to restart in the spring.

J goes out in the early hours with an associate and does a doorway and a few paving stones on Hoe Street. Stencil-and-spray.

Z has been pulled into the union-side/management-side meeting, alongside P. They sit across the table from A, N and G. W is watching A, Z is watching N, and P is watching G (and, it is probably fair to say, vice versa).

Union side collectively has a lean and hungry look. It's the walking, the cycling, the sheer quantity of energy expended upon subterfuge, espionage and counter-espionage.

W always wears a jacket to meetings with management. Not that she feels the need to suit up, but she needs somewhere to hide the mic. P and Z either side of her in shirtsleeves, P's rolled above the elbow.

We want you to stop hacking us, says W.
We're not hacking you, says management side suavely and blandly, in the person of A (hand-stitched Italian suit).

W changes the set of the questions and statements, reeling off request and accusation until she says: And of course we know that Q is a management spy – and the poker face slips momentarily. W sees it slip, Z sees it slip, and P sees it slip (they all compare notes afterwards, and this is what they saw, on the three-headed monster – each of its heads aligned, its reactions congruent, unanimous and legible).

(Only the certain prospect of mutually assured destruction keeps management side from cancelling W's pass and escorting her off the premises with a cardboard box. Or in a cardboard box.)

So Q is the traitor. In the off-site meeting at a pub in Leyton, W, Z and P ponder what to do with her.

W is in touch with K, a shop steward at the Jaguar factory in Coventry. They met on a union residential. She will help him, on condition that he encrypt everything. And maybe he can help them.

★

P's stationery requisition has been queried by management, leaving him without highlighter pens for the foreseeable future, and his Christmas leave request revoked. (Management has correctly identified the weakest link, and is subjecting it to battery.)

Better to die on your feet than live on your knees, says W.

We're dying on our arse here, says P.

Management goon N follows W out of the building at lunchtime and manages to trip up and elbow her off the pavement almost into the path of a passing van. Sorry, he says, and walks on.

From the metadata, M and her colleagues have now identified the members of the Nottingham–Derby hub and worked out the direction of command. They have posited X as the ringleader and applied for a fast-track content search. (They're going to be disappointed when they find out it's a book group gushing over the latest offering from Sunjeev Sahota.)

★

Z switches on his laptop, tapes over the webcam and runs the code that visits recipe sites and mildly racist newspapers. He lets it run in the background for an hour while he packages up some stuff for the Coventry bloke and copies out the union minutes.

38

W, whose preference is for the lo-fi, toggles between the Women's Institute and the *Daily Express*. Her webcam is also masked with five-ply duct tape.

Her Nokia 3310 (PAYG, unregistered, cash-only top-ups, never assembled at home) lies on the bed, its battery Sellotaped to its back. If she needs to make a call she gets on the bus – harder to hit a moving target. Or so she's told.

Everyone's favourite Tory, D, has (presumably) called time on the heart-melting conversations with the former director of Liberty and started them up with the NSA whistleblower. He still believes in the death penalty though. But perhaps not for treason.

String of garlic round his neck, sharpened wooden tent peg in his hand, Snowden stalks the wilds of Siberia, his cry a wind that whistles from the Urals straight to the flattened landscapes and cosy common rooms of Cambridge, UK. He'll be needing that garlic. (Though not, I think, the tent peg.)

What's in the parcel, says the Asian guy in the post office, typing the recipient address onto his screen.
Cycle helmet, says Z, daring the guy to challenge him.
The guy looks at him a half-second longer than necessary, then shrugs, stickers it and puts it behind the counter, looking up to see who's next.

W has a friend who purchases the *Morning Star* from his local newsagent and posts it to her in a plain brown envelope when he's finished with it. Just once every few weeks. He's not daft.

J has developed a new miring code, which visits a random number of right-wing sites for every anarcho-leftist one you click on. You can tailor it for plausibility, so it will do the Dinner Party Tory gamut, or the Alf Garnett gamut. He's working on a Tony Blair gamut. It's self-regulating, he assures his customers, so it won't click on anything dodgy.

The Superego (patent pending) is also J's brainchild. It's basically a filter that blocks you from visiting anything that might be of interest to the authorities. You can override it, but it means you exercise caution.

D uses miring and encryption as a matter of course. (His plug-in is currently browsing the Texas gun laws. That'll keep 'em guessing.)

★

Since she took voluntary redundancy in the latest round of efficiencies, T has been turned down for every job she's applied for. It makes no sense at all – she's not even getting interviews. She phoned up one place the other day pretending to be a supplier and asked switchboard for the name of the new postholder – someone younger and less qualified, according to LinkedIn. It can only be her age – but her sick record is excellent. She still keeps up her subs, so she wonders about getting the union to look into age discrimination for her.

While W is parked outside the cash-and-carry somebody dings her car. The manager's son goes through the CCTV footage with her – she's a regular customer – but they can't get a view of the number plate. He tells her where she can get it hammered out for twenty quid. She reckons she'll live with it.

Z has to remember to get enough cash out for the week – doesn't want the ATMs tracking his movements across the city. He cycles over to Barking, just to use the machine there.

Now that the ticket office has closed it's even more difficult for Y to get her Oyster journeys printed to claim on expenses. She has to remember to do them at the other end. You know you should register this online, says the ticket lady, who seems to recognize her. Save you time.

Posters have gone up about the new tourist Oyster cards. You need your passport or photo ID for those.

A flurry of snow swirls to greet her at the mouth of the Tube.

*

At the start of the new term V offers to give an illustrated talk to the class about the Holi festival, and L has this creeping and slightly sickening realization that she's not Muslim after all. That she's Hindu. (But she *said* she was Bengali! How was L supposed to know? *Are* there even Hindus in Bangladesh?) She'd better not mention it to SLT. She declines the offer, citing timetabling and the national curriculum. V's slow nod of understanding has a touch of the eye-roll in it.

Back in Leytonstone, the link goes live. Z has just looked up O. M shouts out to her team leader, who scrambles across to her desk. Colleagues patting her on the shoulder, team leader looking her in the eye and nodding. This'll be worth something at the April board.

Well apparently there are Hindus in Bangladesh. Who knew?

Z has acquired a typewriter. He puts on some heavy metal and turns up the volume to drown out the keystrokes.

J, together with some associates, is planning a distributed denial-of-service attack, to take place on Thursday, on the Tory party HQ.

Anyway, who's to say a Hindu wouldn't be a terrorist?

Agents of the Security Service supply the black-market shops of Roman Road and Whitechapel with pre-bugged Nokias. (Whatever happened to honour amongst thieves?)

Come to think of it, if you *were* a Muslim terrorist, pretending to be a Hindu would be a really good cover.

★

On Thursday M's team leader takes her out for drinks, to a pub on their respective way home. She asks M about her plans and makes careful reference to going for the next board. Opportunities will be coming up, she says. Project leaders will be needed.

At the anti-fascist vigil Z goes bananas at his friend H, who has sent him something via Dropbox – are you crazy? he says. Are you on glue?
You're fucking paranoid, she says, and she walks away.

As she lets herself in, M wonders about a sideways move into one of the international teams, perhaps on secondment, rather than moving up where she is and getting stuck.

J and his colleagues exchange virtual high-fives after they succeed in bringing down the Tory party site. J celebrates alone, with a midnight spliff.

Z's various phones, batteries, SIM cards and Oyster cards are scattered on his bedside table. His head hurts and he can't actually remember which ones he used yesterday – normally he has a mnemonic for this.

That girl he met last night. He's wondering if her accent seemed a little off – didn't seem to match her clothes and teeth. The teeth a bit too straight to be straight, if you know what I mean. He's trying to remember what he might have said to her.

★

The spooks in Cheltenham clock the status change on the board as they arrive for their morning shift. Not that these things ever come as a surprise.

An algorithm at NatWest Bank has identified a pattern in the planned randomness of Z's cash withdrawals, and triggered a report.

(Interestingly, *algorithm* is derived from the name of بن موسى الخوارزمى محمد – Muhammad ibn Musa al-Khwarizmi – a mathematician-astronomer during the Abbasid Caliphate in ninth-century Baghdad, whose achievements include popularizing the use of algebra and introducing positional notation to the West. Every day a school day, huh?)

A manager looks at it, scanning the cash amounts. Petty drug trade, maybe? Something or nothing. Probably not worth bothering the Met.

Z has had something hot to eat now and is back on track with the Oyster cards, handsets, batteries, SIM cards, ATMs. He tries to tune out the background hum of his spinning plates.

It's mock-Ofsted week. L's head of year sits with a notebook and a tick sheet observing the afternoon session.

On his way home from work V's husband, B, is stopped and searched by the cops under the Terrorism Act. (This is coincidental, and unrelated to L's referrals.) He is amused. You think I'm an Islamist? You know this is a sikha, right? At home he pulls out the carbon copy of the docket to show his wife. No wonder they catch so many crooks, he says.

X is in Nottingham Waterstones. If I like Sunjeev Sahota, what else will I like?

*

J returns home from another early-hours jaunt. Lightening sky and the suggestion of spring in the air.

M wakes from a dream in which she missed a vital clue about Leeds – several clues – and it was all too late. She splashes her face with icy water and looks in the mirror. She's up now, so she might as well get up. She sits with a cup of tea watching it get light.

In Syria it is light already. An MSF nurse in Idlib supervises the setting up of a new facility.

The *Morning Star* arrives in Silvertown. W flicks through it before leaving for work.

In Moscow, trained assassins are briefed on the known recent and likely future movements of the NSA whistleblower. His need to keep himself in the public eye – the only thing that will keep him alive – is also his Achilles heel.

W says to Z, I think that Snowden has been dead for quite some time. They're good at this, the Russians, she says. Ventriloquizing. You don't think he runs his own accounts, do you?

I reckon I'll take a bullet one day, she says. (They are sitting on a park bench, eating their lunch.) Well, not a *bullet*, she says. It'll be an accident of some kind, away from work. Gas leak or something.

That's the trouble, she says. It's people like us who do it, people with no family. No one to cry for us when we're gone. No one to look for our bodies.

Inside the Doughnut, coffee at hand, M watches an onscreen transcript of Z's movements. W has been identified as a close contact, and a file opened.

Z watches the clock: just another hour of captivity.

V looks the social workers up and down and tells them to come back with legal paperwork. And she slams the door.

As Z leaves for home, he places a bar of vending-machine chocolate on W's keyboard.

(Oh, Edward, they promised not to torture you – and you believed them, didn't you? What a difference an election makes.)

F, whose ex-husband used to laugh at her refusal to sign petitions, watches the news with a glass of wine and the smug satisfaction of one whom history has proved right. (She was also right, let the record reflect, about the living room walls.)

U and I watch the *Newsnight* special, with increasing unease.

Dawn breaks on a snow plain in the east, revealing a silver whistle, a few drops of blood (see how bright the red against the white and silver!), a petal of garlic peel, an efficient absence of footprints.

BELTANE

The hedgerows are bright with may along the Portsmouth Road. Melanie gets out the flask from the bag at her feet and gingerly pours black coffee.

'Don't drink it all,' says Pete.

Cold air rushes in from the window, not unpleasantly.

'Let's stop for a minute,' she says.

Pete sits with the door open and a leg sticking out, drinking coffee and checking the printout of directions. Melanie stands outside eating a croissant. She licks the crumbs from her fingers and crouches to wash her hands in the dew, then her face.

The daisies have woken. Mel picks a few, then reaches up to snap off an umbel of elder, tucking it behind her ear.

'You've smudged your eyeliner,' says Pete, pulling back onto the road.

Melanie shrugs. She peers in the vanity mirror to repair it a little, then strings her daisies, holding them at elbow length like a grandmother threading a needle.

Pete glances over at her.

'What? I don't need reading glasses.'

★

Off the A3 there is nothing but fields and sky. White blossom everywhere. Twisting roads. Waxed-jacket territory. Stretchy clouds.

They park a short way away and walk up a mud track. They can hear music (bagpipes, even?) distantly. There is no security or gating, which surprises them.

As they round the corner into the field they see a procession approaching from the woodlands at the far end, maybe a hundred people, winding a slow path down towards them, with chants and percussion and yes, bagpipes, a stout blonde in a long white dress at the head of it. The processants appear to be carrying a maypole.

Along the boundary, an advance party of small children is hitting the hedges with sticks. Pete raises an eyebrow.

Nearby and to their right is a first-aid tent, and what looks to be a drinks marquee. Further up, a row of Portaloos. The field is otherwise empty, except for a bunch of people in the middle capering about on hobbyhorses.

They make for the drinks marquee – above the entrance, a hand-painted sign saying 'Cakes and Ale'.

'Welcome,' says a bearded crusty in a jester's hat and motley, some kind of pelt across his shoulders. 'Have you come far?'

'London,' says Mel.

'Twice welcome. First time?'

They nod. His voice has a Hampshire burr.

'Try the local brew?'

'Go on then,' says Pete.

'I'll have a cake too,' says Mel, pointing.

'These are special cakes. Best not sampled if you're driving.'

'Gotcha. I'll have the other sort.'

'Keep hold of your cup for refills and bring it back to the bins at the end. Enjoy.'

They wander back out to where the hobbyhorses are, spread their travel rug on the grass, still damp with dew, and drink their beer. The procession is now at the bottom corner of the field, enacting some ritual. Some of the celebrants are rolling in the dew. Others are taking off jackets and jumpers and shirts, turning them inside out and putting them on again. The blonde presides, her arms aloft, repeating an indeterminate chant. A few obvious tourists bring up the rear, watching the proceedings but not joining in. The children continue to work their way down the field, battering the hedges.

A young woman riding a hobbyhorse circles Mel and Pete, whinnying and nickering. 'Hello,' says Pete.

More visitors arrive, settling down with rugs or investigating the drinks tent, emerging with plastic quarts of cider and cakes of one or the other variety.

The procession makes a diagonal towards them. The blonde is wearing a tall crown of hawthorn, a girdle belt of meadow flowers and a sash appliquéd with the legend 'Queen of the May'. The train of her long white gown is muddied and her hair frizzy. Her eyelids are caked with blue shadow.

The horses stop their capering and back into a circle as the Queen approaches, only rearing occasionally.

The Queen raises a hand and the maypole bearers come forward, adolescent boys in satin britches and jerkins and tricorn hats in varying shades of blue. They raise the maypole, as the mast of a sailboat might be raised. The pole is topped with a crown of flowers.

A recorder quartet, all in Elizabethan costume, steps out and begins to play. Dancers in hooped skirts and floral coronets leave the procession and station themselves around the pole, alternating with the satin boys. The oldest boy, dressed all in lavender, hands out the streamers.

The women dance clockwise and the boys anticlockwise, weaving in and out of the ribbons, which plait as the dance wears on, red and white, red and white, pulling them in to the pole.

The lavender boy looks like he stepped off a village green in 1560. His hair is worn long in a pageboy cut, the same as the other boys. They are clearly all siblings, or cousins.

The dark-haired middle boy is in turquoise and the youngest and blondest in baby blue. Now they are plaiting a kind of tent, some of the dancers standing still and the others weaving between them.

The dance finishes and the lavender boy steps out, takes Mel's arm and steers her to a place. His eyes are lavender too. One of the other dancers has captured Pete. The music starts and the dance begins, sunwise, a simple skipping round the pole. Mel's elderflower falls out of her ear and is trodden on by the dancer behind, who mouths 'sorry' with a grin. She can't stop to pick it up but then sees the Cakes and Ale barman reach in from the crowd and pluck it from under the trampling feet. As she passes him again he smiles at her, holding the flower to his chin.

On the other side of the pole, Pete has a good skipping action. When the dance ends, the barman approaches and holds out the slightly crushed elder to her.

'Find Patti,' he says. 'She'll help you make a crown.'

'Patti's up by the bales,' says someone. 'They're making them there.'

Up towards the wood, Mel and Pete find a woman who must be Patti, sitting on a hay bale resplendent in medieval robes and occult pendants, her greying hair in a bun. A pile of besom brooms and a line of metal buckets filled with water rest near her. She is drinking from a clay cup.

'We'll be lighting them soon,' she says, as they approach. 'Just waiting for the fire.' She nods over her right shoulder, near the uppermost corner of the field, where a small group huddles round a shallow pit.

'We want to make crowns,' says Mel.

'Oh, I'll do some of that later. Here it comes.'

A young woman in a rainbow jumper runs over with a flaming torch.

'Stand back,' says Patti, and touches the torch to a bale, corner by corner. It catches quickly. 'We'll do the others once there's a crowd.'

The flames soon draw a small one away from the maypole, and after a while the dancing music stops.

'Who's for jumping?' says Patti. She takes a broomstick and gives one end to the rainbow girl. They hold it four feet in the air like a high jump and Patti extends her other hand in invitation. A tall man steps forward. As soon as he does so, they raise the broom to five feet, nearly over the girl's head. The crowd laughs, and so does the man. He takes a step back, then a couple more, patting the crowd back with his hands, then hurls himself over the jump shoulders first like an Olympian. The crowd applauds.

'Any more?' says Patti.

Mel steps forward and gets a cheer. Patti and the girl raise the jump and duck slightly as Mel crashes sideways over it, landing with a roll and flattening her elderflower again. Patti takes Mel's wrist and holds it up in the air and the crowd cheers more loudly. Mel notices the Cakes and Ale barman in the midst, nodding and applauding.

The hay bale blazes behind the women. Patti holds up a finger, then relights the torch. She touches it to a fresh bale. A man puts his arm up and comes forward. He takes a step and leaps the burning bale. Another follows.

Mel pushes Pete in the centre of his back. 'Are you bloody mad?' he says. 'I'm not doing it.'

'Oh go on, I'd try it myself but I don't want to singe my DMs.'

The flames dance higher. The lavender boy pushes through the crowd, takes off his hat and jerkin, gives them to an audience member to hold, rolls up the sleeves of his shirt and splashes his hose and britches with water. He wets his hair with his hands and tucks it behind his ears. He looks at the bale.

'Go on then,' shouts someone. 'Get on with it.'

Lavender Boy looks at the heckler and smiles. He goes back to the bucket and splashes some more.

'That's polyester,' hisses Mel. 'It'll go up like a Christmas tree. Someone'll have to stop him.' And she looks around her.

But the crowd cheers and eggs him on. Pete puts a hand on Mel's arm as Lavender Boy jumps the bale, well above the flames, and then jumps back again, just before the hay dissolves into fire. He reclaims his hat and jerkin, raises his hat in the air for further applause before putting it on, and then jogs damply back to the maypole.

The crowd begins to jostle and push men forward as Patti raises her torch high above another bale.

Pete hoists the picnic rucksack and gestures to a clear and sunlit spot of green towards the hedgerow. As they spread their lunch out on the rug and finish off the coffee they can hear the sound of near misses over at the balefires. At one point there is a commotion of buckets and shouts. They stand up to get a look but can't see anything.

'They're probably used to it.' Mel unlaces her boots and lets the cool breeze onto her feet.

Across the field she spots some of the costumed dancers going in and out of a trailer near the beer tent, loitering in the doorway with cups of tea. One of the hoop-skirted women is pacing around the back, cigarette in hand, making a call on a mobile. The field is filling up with picnickers. The maypole music has begun again, slower and more mournful – an Elizabethan dirge or a tale of lost love. The dancers step slowly and deliberately, circling one another with measured paces, turning away from each other, clapping their free hands together and swapping ribbons between them, perfectly in time.

'Do you think they make a living out of it?' she says. 'Family business?'

'It's a little seasonal, isn't it,' says Pete.

Mel stands. Free of her 14-hole DMs, her feet breathe in the soft grass. She runs a hand along the hedgerow and disturbs a small bird. The neighbouring meadow is alive with butterflies.

Further along she finds a gap in the hedge and slips through to the other side. A man with binoculars nods at her and carries on. The earth is dry and hard on her feet and the flowers almost waist-height already. The music and chatter behind her get quieter as she walks, and she can hear insects in the grasses. Towards the wood a cloud of midges and dragonflies hovers over a faint smell of damp. There are people in the wood too – she can hear activity now that it's not drowned out by the noise of the field, and occasionally see a movement in the trees.

The sky is a cloudless cyan. In the background the hills roll above a green cornfield, and if she crouches down, the human sounds are muffled by the thick vegetation and by the buzzing and the thrumming near her ears.

When Pete comes to find her, she is lying in the long grass, clasping a bunch of oxeye daisies to her chest.

'For a crown,' she says.

They sit in the meadow for a while, looking at the hills.

On their way back to the field they stop at the hedge and pick buds of elder and crab apple.

The campfire at the pit is glowing brightly when they emerge. Patti is there, on an upturned bucket, fashioning some pliant branches into a hoop.

A man in a denim shirt and an unadorned wicker crown is drumming quietly. He acknowledges them as they sit down, then closes his eyes and continues to play.

A plump cross-legged woman chucks them over lengths of willow, dogwood and ivy from a pile on a piece of sacking in front of her. Around the circle people weave crowns and whittle bits of wood. A red-headed teenager sits still as a woman braids sections of her hair into tiny plaits, folding in cow parsley and sprays of forget-me-nots and ears of unripe barley, roping them into a crown.

Melanie takes a stem of catkinned willow and works it into a round, sizing it on her head and binding it with ivy and grasses and the bloom she picked from the roadside this morning.

Patti nods approvingly. 'The weaving together of two substances to form a third,' she says. 'It's a powerful magick.' Melanie can hear the final 'k' in her intonation.

She twists the elder and oxeye daisies into the willow, knotting them individually round the base and winding them tight.

Pete makes a wand, choosing a rowan branch and stripping the leaves from its length.

Mel tests her crown on her head.

'It's good,' says the woman plaiting hair. 'Very natural.'

The afternoon is hot. Mel rolls up her sleeves to the shoulders and loosens the buttons at the top and bottom of her dress. Pete rolls his jeans to the calf. They lie on the grass. The rainbow girl, minus her jumper, in a white short-sleeved T-shirt, begins to strum a guitar.

The redhead now has a thick rope of hair coiled around her head, studded with grasses and barley and clouds of blue and white flowers.

They watch the line for the beer tent, which shows no sign of abating. Pete takes their cups and goes off to queue.

A side of Morris men has started up just past the hay bales, jumping in air to clash batons and hit each other with bladders. It looks too energetic for the heat.

Turquoise Boy and Little Boy Blue stroll past, Little Boy Blue eating something from a paper bag.

The barman appears at the fireside. He's taken off his pelt and jester's hat, revealing collar-length fair hair turning to grey, and wears a garland of wild flowers over his motley. He is carrying an army kitbag and a metal stockpot.

'Patti,' he says.

'Chris,' says Patti.

He crouches down, takes a stick, checks it over and stokes the bonfire with it.

He rubs his hands and holds them to the heat.

He looks up at Mel. 'It's a good crown,' he says. 'Isn't it, Patti?'

Mel straightens it on her head.

'Oh yes,' says Patti. 'It's a good 'un.'

'Where's that man of yours?' he says to Mel.

'Getting drinks.'

He lies down on his side and props his head on his hand. She notices his britches are inside out.

'Gonna get that cauldron on, Chris?' says Patti.

'In good time,' he says. Then, to the cross-legged plump woman, 'Chuck us some willow, Becky.'

She does so, placidly, and he winds it into a crown, looking at Mel all the while.

'Don't fall asleep wearing that one,' he says to her.

'Why?'

He stretches out a hand and touches it.

'Made of elder. The *aos sí*'ll have you.' He looks up. 'Hello mate.'

Pete puts a quart bottle of cider down on the ground. 'Hello,' he says.

Chris sits up.

'Cider?' says Pete. 'Have you got a cup?'

Chris pulls a plastic one out of his kitbag. 'Just a bit,' he says, as Pete shares the bottle into thirds.

Pete lies on the ground beside Mel, propped on an elbow.

'I'll get the cauldron on,' says Chris, kneeling up.

He takes a stick and rakes some of the glowing logs to the edge of the firepit, then stands the stockpot on them, balancing it with stones and poking in grasses for kindling. From the kitbag he unpacks a bunch of dried lavender, a tub full of small clay cups, a ladle and several corked glass bottles of straw-coloured liquid.

He empties two of the bottles carefully into the cauldron.

'Is that a wand?' he says to Pete.

Pete hands him the wand, and he uses it to stir the liquid.

'Thanks,' he says, and hands it back.

He crumbles lavender on top and replaces the lid at an angle.

Taking up his crown again, he laces it with apple blossom and rowan, with the oxeye daisies – but not the elder – Mel has discarded. He has a self-made tattoo, possibly an occult symbol, on the back of his hand.

The circle widens a little to admit newcomers, amongst them the three maypole boys. Now they are sitting together it's clear they are brothers. Some kind of genius has matched their costumes to the colours of their eyes.

The eldest has taken off his jerkin again. His lawn shirt is open at the throat, his throat almost pale as the shirt.

Turquoise Boy's face is freckled and ruddier than the others. There's something more knowing in his look as he meets Mel's now. She stretches and turns away.

Chris has finished his crown and is wearing it. The white and pink of the blossom sets off the blond of his hair. He smiles at her.

He opens the cauldron again and stirs it, dredging up a ladleful and letting it pour back in. The liquid is beginning to smoke. He takes a clay cup and ladles out a measure, then tips it into the fire, which flares bright green. He refills the cup and offers it to Pete.

'Driving,' says Pete.

Mel accepts the drink. It's sweet and thick and heady. The clay of the cup is fired but unglazed, still bearing fingerprints of the maker.

Chris carries on filling cups and passing them round the circle. Nearly everyone takes one, including the teenagers. He uncorks another two bottles and tips them into the cauldron, sprinkling in lavender and stirring again with the wand.

He stokes the bonfire, seriously now, untying bundles of sticks, retying them in small bunches and stacking them against the flames, burning his fingers. Turquoise Boy helps build the fire and pack in kindling.

More people are joining the circle, rolling what are left of the hay bales over as an outer row and sitting atop them. Joints are passed around small groups. Their corner of the field is becoming crowded. Mel sees a huge dragonfly above their heads, with pleasure at first, then as it flits back and forth across the circle and she realizes it's lost, rising panic. It will die here, she thinks. Like a trapped bird battering itself out in a room. Her heart beats fast and high.

She takes a breath involuntarily and the smoke from the campfire hits the back of her throat and her eyes fill.

Pete is talking to the red-headed girl. Chris takes Mel's wrist, circling it with a thumb and finger. She closes her eyes. When she opens them again the dragonfly is gone.

Next to Mel and Chris, Rainbow picks up her jumper, turns it inside out and puts it back on again. 'Dusk coming,' she says to them with a nod. 'Don't want to forget.'

More bales and logs are brought to form another row of the circle. Mel recognizes the recorder quartet from earlier with some of the Morris men, who appear to be playing a drinking game. The female recorder player, dressed like a principal boy, now carries a ukulele. Across the field the maypole lies dormant, its ribbons coiled.

Chris refills her cup, touches her lightly on the back and goes to rebuild the fire.

Lavender Boy looks at the sky, mutters something to his brother and takes off his shirt. From the other side of the circle, Pete looks at Mel with narrowed eyes. The boy unhurriedly turns the sleeves inside out and then sits by the fire holding them for a while, flames reflecting on his pale torso.

Pete creeps back across to Mel. 'Go on,' he says at her ear. 'Ask him about his maypole.'

'Shut up.'

The boy puts the shirt back on, inside out.

'Show's over. How disappointing.' He whispers in her ear again. 'Do you think he's a virgin?'

'Oh shut it now.'

'He's got lovely eyes, have you noticed?'

She hits him in the chest with her forearm and he laughs and moves away.

Bluegrass music drifts across the circle as the shadows fall. Some of the men from the bales are helping to build up the fire, discussing the stacking of wood. They ask the inner circle to move back a little, and everyone shuffles accordingly.

A huntshorn sounds from the forest. Mel hears it with a coursing of adrenaline, a reflex from her sabbing days. A few people look up and at each other, as if scenting something.

Chris goes to his kitbag and produces ritual kit – an antlered headdress, a veil, a cloak. He steps over the edge of the fire and crouches next to Mel.

'Will you be the maiden?' he says.

'What?'

'The maiden. In the dance.'

'Oh. I'll be forty in August.'

He shrugs. 'I'm much older than that.'

'I wouldn't have guessed,' she says politely.

He nods. 'It's the May dew.'

The horn sounds again. He looks up. 'They're coming.'

The Queen and some woad-streaked courtiers emerge from the forest, some shirtless and carrying torches. Around the circle people start drumming. Pete looks at Mel and moves closer to her. The courtiers shake blossomed branches in time to the drums. Their eyes are hectic.

'Pinned,' says Pete.

'Not the queen,' says Mel.

'No, not her. But the others.'

The Queen's face is smeared with charcoal, and some of her eyeshadow has come off. Her hair is frizzier than ever.

Chris stands. He is wearing a heavy mantle, and his pelt over it. He carries the horned headdress, the veil and the cloak.

The circle breaks to let the Queen through.

'The axis of the earth is increasing its tilt relative to the sun,' she shouts, her voice big and hoarse, and everyone cheers and pummels their drums and shakes their branches.

'She's got a pair of lungs on her, hasn't she?' says Pete.

'We shall be blessed with abundance this year.' She flings her arms skyward.

'It sounds like a threat.'

'And we welcome the Horned God, king of the forest.' She throws out an arm and there is Chris, wearing the headdress. The cheering and drumming crescendoes. The female recorder player gives the loudest wolf-whistle Mel has ever heard, and the Morris men wave their sticks and bells in the air.

'I need a woman,' shouts Chris. There is laughter. His eyes fall on Mel.

'Melanie,' says Pete.

The Queen, too, looks at Mel. 'A woman in her childbearing years who is not yet a mother,' she shouts, and takes a step towards her. Around the circle the gaze travels towards Mel.

'Melanie…' says Pete, and grips her arm, but Mel gets up.

The Queen holds out a mantle to her and fastens it around her shoulders. It reaches to the ground and the hem is weighted.

'The fire won't burn you,' says Chris.

'Sit down,' says the Queen to Pete. Rainbow pulls him back down again. The Queen and her courtiers attach the veil to Mel's head and replace her crown.

The Queen takes off her own appliquéd sash and slips it over Mel's head.

'Walk on the edge of the fire,' says Chris. 'Just on the edge.'

'What about my boots,' she says, and tries to avoid the embers.

She leans experimentally into the flames for a moment. The mantle doesn't catch.

'Mind your hair,' says the Queen, quietly.

The Queen lights a torch in the fire and raises it above her head. 'Now is the time,' she shouts.

Around the circle there is a flurry of people taking off jackets and shirts and putting them back on again. The Morris men reverse their waistcoats.

Patti takes the cauldron off the fire and ladles out cups. She hands a cake to the Queen, who lights it in the flames and hands it back. Patti breaks off and distributes the smouldering crumbs. Around the circle people eat and drink.

The innermost row leans away as Mel circles the fire, swinging her mantle. It catches someone in the chin.

'Beltane is here!' the Queen shouts at the crowd. 'Beltane is here!' And then she points her torch at Chris, brushing him with the flames. He moves only when they get close to his face – and the Queen laughs.

'He is the god of the forest,' she bellows. 'He is known by many names. Pan, Herne, Cernunnos, the Green Man. He is the god of the forest and at sundown he will capture the Maiden.'

The horn sounds again.

The Queen turns to Mel. 'RUN.' She laughs as Mel tries to escape the circle. The crowd pushes her back in.

'She is the Queen of the May... Ceridwen... goddess of the fields and flowers. She is... *Mother Earth herself*,' shouts the Queen as Mel runs round the fire.

Mel's lungs are protesting and the blood drums in her ears. She can't hear the Queen's words any more. She is dizzy from running in a circle and breathing in smoke. She sways and almost falls into the fire. Someone pulls her out again and pushes her forward but she can't run any further. She stops. Around the circle the drumming and shouting stops and everyone is still. They all look at her, flames reflected in their faces. The Queen takes a step towards her, fixing her with her eyes. So does the horned god.

She looks into his eyes. There is a crackle of electricity as she takes his outstretched hand. They step around the fire and he takes her other hand too and they walk through it. The crowd cheers. He leans into her ear and whispers.

He lets go her hands, lifts the headdress over his head, scans the circle for Pete and holds it out to him. Hands from the crowd push Pete forward. Pete takes the headdress and puts it on. The crowd screams and whistles.

'What did he say?' says Pete, under cover of the shouting.

Mel shakes her head.

The drumming begins again.

Mel looks at Pete. She begins to walk round the fire and so does he. She reaches out to take his hand and feels the snap of the current again. She looks in his eyes and there is something like fear there; it pulses through their fingers. Over his shoulder she sees a blurred shape like his shadow but larger.

When the drumming stops, Pete takes off his antlers. Slowly people begin to clap, and the Queen steps forward again and takes their hands in hers for a moment and then turns to the crowd with arms raised. Mel removes her veil and cloak, both smudged with ash.

Pete takes her arm. 'I felt it,' he says. 'Did you?'

'Must be the ley lines.'

Chris comes over to them, holding the headdress under his arm like a severed head. 'Will you stay for the burning?' he says.

'Work tomorrow,' says Pete.

A flicker of disappointment passes across the face of the horned god.

'We'd better get going, actually,' Pete says to Mel, glancing at the sky as Patti approaches and hands Chris a mead cup and he turns to her.

There is a small gathering by the Portaloos, standing well back as if by a cashpoint. Mel waits in line.

Already Venus is shining over the black trees, a tiny paring of a moon just visible in the still-bright day.

The bar is shut and the field deserted again, except for the mass of people round the fire. In the shadows by the empty tent she sees Lavender Boy with the red-headed girl. He clocks her and moves away.

The other queuers disappear into Portaloos and suddenly Mel is alone. The dew has fallen. She lies down and rolls in it, three times clockwise and three anticlockwise. She stands and meets the turquoise eyes of Turquoise Boy, who is sitting on the steps of his trailer.

'Your time will come,' she calls out over to him. Another Portaloo door swings open. She jams her crown on her head and exits into it.

Pete is outside waiting for her. He points to the woods. An effigy is being borne down towards the campfire, as the maypole was earlier borne. The cheering and drumming and whooping begin again, figures standing on the bales and falling off them.

They take their recycling to the bins, piled high above their heads to overflowing with crushed plastic cups and quart bottles.

They take a last look back at the effigy, then leave the field, walking down the mud track to the car. The sun is sinking now, and the hedgerows dark.

'Should've brought a torch,' says Pete.

A collection of cars lines the track and clumps at the foot of it. Theirs is almost boxed in. A girl in a hi-vis jacket gets up from a chair, waves at them and directs them out.

Mel looks over at the hills. In the light of the setting sun she can see the three brothers wandering on the edge of the cornfield, the younger ones hatless, their hair and their faces catching the last rays. She can almost forget that their costumes are polyester. When she looks again a minute later, they are gone.

Pylons bestride the fields like wicker men as the old gold lights the Downs.

'Let's call in sick,' says Pete. 'Stick it to The Man.'

'Thought you weren't drinking.'

He runs a hand over his face.

'Let's stop for a minute,' he says.

They drive north and east, away from the sun, towards the new moon. From the windows, the smell of dusk.

THE BIRD

'Caz.'

She can never, ever wake up in her own time. He's nudging her now, shaking her shoulder, and some displaced pain, some icy chip of something, is rattling in her head.

'Hhhhm.' It's more a swatting away.

She did sleep a little – an hour or two maybe. He slept on the coach to the airport, on the plane, and nearly all the way from Gatwick to Brighton. She'd fought sleep, succumbing some time after Crawley and waking up just after they'd missed their stop.

'Caz, I think there's a bird in the room.'

She feels like digging her nails into his arm, giving him a Chinese burn. 'Must be outside. Go to sleep.'

'Listen.'

She drags herself up out of half sleep. Her whole body aches with the effort. The room is looking cold and grey and the sheets are dirty and freezing. A huge pile of presents lies in the middle of the floor.

'It's nothing. Go back to sleep.' She pulls the pillow around her ears.

He pulls it back. 'Listen.'

She hears a muffled flurry and then a slight thump. She knows this sound. The last time the landlord had done the gas safety inspections, the gasman had pulled a dead pigeon out of the chimney. 'Wanna look?' 'Eucch, no.' He'd chuckled, an older man.

'Oh god.'

'What?'

'It's a pigeon down the chimney.'

'What can we do?'

'Nothing. Go back to sleep.'

An hour later she wakes again to the sound of scuffling behind the gas fire. The windows are rattling and the top of her head's cold. She remembers the bird.

She gets out of bed, pulls on a jumper and goes into the kitchen. The sky is white. In the fortnight since they've been gone the weather's turned and the leaves have started to fall. Her bouquet's on the worktop, sitting in green water in a jam jar. It's going mouldy and starting to smell sweet and rotten. Even the ribbon is mouldy. His buttonhole too – they'd meant to hang it upside down, dry it out, but they'd forgotten in the hurry.

She takes sliced bread from the freezer compartment and makes toast and black coffee. When she brings the tray into the studio room he's awake again, all eyelashes and languor. He eats the toast.

'Is it still in there?'

She looks at him. 'Yes.'

'Will it be able to get out?'

'No. I'm going to have a shower.'

She closes her eyes and lifts up her head in the shower, washing the grime of the sheets, and the coach and the plane and the airport and the coach and the sand and the suntan oil off her.

After lunch they unpack their cases and take the washing down to the laundrette and, while they're there, ask about dry-cleaning prices. They pick up juice, milk, bread, a chicken and vegetables. They spend the afternoon sorting through a carrier bag of cards, reading out messages to each other, pulling out money and vouchers and laying them in separate piles on the carpet. Caz notes down on a pad of paper who gave what.

They go to the bank and pay in all the money bar a few notes, into Caz's account. They pay the invoices that have arrived while they've been away.

The presents are still heaped in the middle of the floor, silver and white and blue. Caz hoovers around them.

They cook a nice dinner of chicken and vegetables, carry it through to the studio room, turn the lights on and sit down on the sofa to eat it. He opens one of the bottles of wine left over from the wedding.

As soon as they put the first forkful to their mouths there's a tap from behind the gas fire. Tap, tap, tap. A pause. They listen. Then more insistently, assertively: TAP, TAP, TAP.

He puts down his fork. 'It's almost as if it knows we're here.'

Tap, tap, tap.

She is silent. She realizes, and maybe he does too, that it does know they are there. That from its dark prison it can see the chinks of electric light through the joins in the boarded-up fireplace, and through the gaps where the fire's plumbed in. That it can see an escape route. That it can hear them talking.

He says, 'I wonder how long it's been there.'

'It could have been there for days.'

'How long can they live like that?'

'How should I know?'

She pushes her food around and leaves most of it – a waste of a good chicken. Later, after washing up, they sit in the tiny kitchen to finish their wine, but the carcass in the lidless bin and the bones on the plates remind Caz of the pigeon.

They sit up late in the kitchen. When they go to bed the room's quiet but Caz wakes in the night and hears scrabbling. It's quieter though, and then it stops. She strains her ears to hear: there is nothing. She wonders if that's it. And then it starts again. She blocks up her ears with the pillow. She thinks she can hear it through the feathers of the pillow.

The next day after a late brunch they decide to open the presents. There are bewilderingly many. They take turns.

Caz sets out the strategy. After each present they open they will make a note of the item and any distinguishing features (colour, pattern) and the giver (full name). The person who opens the present will be responsible for recording it. They will put the unwrapped presents in a clean storage box. They will not deviate from this plan.

Silver tissue paper yields a boxed china cake stand, the type found in old-fashioned tea shops and flea markets ('Beautiful,' sighs Caz). There's a tea set, an Indian tablecloth and napkins, a lead crystal vase, a bottle of port and a set of port glasses, a cocktail shaker, some doilies, a sushi set, a cheese bell, various items of cookware, including a blender and heart-shaped cookie cutters, some framed photographs of Brighton, and a lot of booze.

There are more cards taped to the presents – thick, square, pastel-coloured envelopes which scatter sequins or glitter when they are opened. Some of the boxed presents have come detached from their cards (or never had cards?) And maybe some cards in the presents pile never had presents attached. The two of them scour the wrappings for a clue. In some cases they find a loose matching gift tag or a note written directly onto the wrapping. In the end they have three loose cards and two loose presents – the tea set and a bottle of Tuaca. The Tuaca has a gift tag but no signature. Neither of them recognizes the handwriting. They check it against the loose cards but it doesn't match. The tea set has no gift tag.

They dig out the guest list. They cross off all the people whose gifts could be identified. Then they divide the people remaining into two categories – people who might have given the tea set and people who might have given the Tuaca.

They think they have identified the tea set giver. They make a few guesses about the Tuaca. This process, punctuated by sandwiches and tapping, takes all afternoon. It seems a shame to put all the shiny sequinned paper into the recycling, but they do this.

Turning the lamp on provokes a long series of taps, so they turn it off again and sit in the gloom. This doesn't stop the tapping but it becomes more intermittent.

They can't face another evening of listening to the bird dying. They go into town, to a vegetarian restaurant in the Lanes, to escape.

They stay as late as they dare, eking out a slab of chocolate cake between them in tiny forkfuls. They smile at each other across the table, thinking of all the evenings spent in unwalled restaurants with plastic red-and-white check tablecloths, sharing out the last of the carafe as behind them the staff unobtrusively stacked chairs and wiped down the bar.

Caz pulls out the wad of wedding money and fans it with her thumb.

'Better get the bill.'

It's starting to spit with rain as they walk home.

It's cold in the studio room, but they daren't put the fire on. The room is quiet and still. Caz rubs her hands and turns the small lamp on. They lie on the floor by the fire even though it's unlit.

She rolls a cigarette. She's rolling up the cocktails by the pool of the last evening, in the stars on the beach of the last night, scooping in the stray crabs they saw scuttle across wet dark sand in the moonlight.

He's watching her hands as she rolls, as she strikes a match that flares in the dark, the new gold ring that was his grandmother's catching its light.

'Can I have one?' He reaches out and touches her hair with his fingertips.

She takes one more drag and blows out the smoke. 'You can finish this one. I don't want it.'

She lies on her back on the floor with her hands behind her head, looking up at the ceiling, seeing the starry sky.

And then there's a thud and a rattling that makes her jump as the pigeon hurls itself against the back of the fireplace. And then the tapping begins again. Caz counts more than thirty taps. Maybe it was the smoke that roused it. They get up off the floor.

He says, 'I suppose there's nothing one can do?'

'Short of ripping the fireplace out.'

'Could we do that?' He starts feeling along the glued joins of the board.

'No. Just come to bed.'

The tapping stops once they turn the lamp out, but it's soon replaced by scraping and flurrying that continues into the early hours – flurrying more and more frantic, and occasionally an echoing clang as the whole fireplace shakes. Perhaps it goes on all night. They fall asleep eventually from exhaustion, when it's already starting to get light. She wakes a couple of hours later needing the loo and then lies awake for an hour or more looking at the wedding dress and suit still hanging up in their body bags on the wardrobe, and listening to the rain and the beating of wings.

On the third morning they're up early, feeling groggy and sandy-eyed, and she makes a breakfast of toast and raspberry jam. He has to go to work in the afternoon. As soon as they sit on the sofa to eat, it starts: five taps, louder than ever and more insistent. It sounds like a hammer. She imagines its beak all smashed and bloody. She pushes away the toast and jam. He can't eat either. The tapping goes on. It sounds as though it's trying to chip its way out.

'Let's rip out the fireplace,' she says.

'Can we do that?'

'I don't know. Let's give it a go.'

He looks pleased at this, hopeful.

'We need to turn off the gas at the mains and then get to where the fire's plumbed in and work from there,' she says. 'We need to pull the fire away from the wall without bursting the pipes.'

'You turn the gas off and I'll move the fire out.'

'Be careful not to burst the pipes or we'll have a leak.'

She goes into the hallway to find the gas tap. 'Don't move until I say so.' She turns it off at the emergency valve. 'Ready.' She hears the casing of the fire judder out a few inches. 'Be careful not to burst the pipes.'

'Sweetie, I think this is going to be easier than we thought.'

More scraping of metal.

'Mind those pipes,' she calls, and then she hears him take a breath. 'What? What is it?'

More scraping.

'Caz – come in here a sec.'

'What is it?' She moves to the doorway.

'Caz, it's a gull.'

'What?'

'I think so. Caz, come and see. Come and check.'

She approaches, sees the letterbox-sized hole behind the fire, the flue, and inside it a face.

'Oh no no no.'

A clear yellow eye, a yellow beak, an unmistakeable profile. Just its face, with its eye looking at them. They look back.

'Is there anything we can feed it?' he says doubtfully, peering through the letterbox.

'We have to get it out.'

He wrenches the gas fire out a little more. He can't pull it right out because the pipes will burst. The letterbox hole is cut into a piece of metal sheeting, about ten inches square. This metal square is sealed with gaffer tape. 'How are we going to do this?'

'We need something to catch it in, so we can get it downstairs. And you need to put something on in case it attacks you.'

They settle on a cagoule, sunglasses and a pair of Marigold gloves for him, and the Indian tablecloth to catch the gull in. It watches them, calm now: no longer moving, no longer pecking.

He kneels down by the fire. 'The trouble is, we don't know what state it's in.'

He peels away a strip of the gaffer tape. The gull jumps at the sound. She wanders back into the hallway. A wave of nausea hits her. She hears the ripping of another strip and then the metal sheet being pulled away from the cavity.

Then, 'Hello, sweetie. Alright, sweetie.'

Metallic scuffling. It won't stay in there, won't let him free it properly. It's trying to squeeze its way through that tiny gap. She imagines it pressing its flesh against the unfiled edges, beads of blood appearing on its feathered breast. He's holding out the

Indian tablecloth, trying to help it. Outside the room she moans and covers her face, a taste of pennies in her mouth.

'It's no use flapping, sweetie.'

She realizes he's talking to her now, not the bird.

A muscular flap and a clang of metal. She can see the blood in her mind. She can't look. And then a flurry.

'Caz. Caz. Look.'

She comes back to the doorway.

And it's on her desk. Dirty. Grey. Of course – it's been in a chimney for forty-eight hours. Otherwise whole. No bleeding or visible damage. A seagull. Standing in the middle of her room. It looks at them both with its clear eye, stands its ground.

'I need a box. The recycling box.'

She runs down the hall and he hears her empty it onto the floor, tin cans rolling away on the lino and bottles clinking.

He leans over to catch the gull. It escapes, springs onto the television. He's stalking it, menacing it with the box. It doesn't mean to be trapped again.

'I think you'll have to grab it. Like a chicken.'

He misses. It's in the hallway.

'Or herd it out of doors.'

He tries. It's going the wrong way, to the flat upstairs. He grabs it. He's got it. He runs down the stairs with it, shouting over his shoulder.

'Out, out, out – open the doors, open the doors.'

She runs ahead of him, opens the doors. And it's out. He's put it down outside, on the wet front steps. The rain's starting again, very gently. The grey gull looks doddery, looking up, to left and right, in the bright morning air. Dazzled, it looks like it's forgotten what the world is. It puts up its head to catch water.

'Shall I get it some water?'

73

He shakes his head. 'No. No need.'

'I'll get it some water.'

She runs inside and upstairs. When she comes down again with a bowl, her husband is on the other side of the road.

She calls from the doorway. 'Where's the gull?'

He points to the gate pillar of the house opposite.

'Is that ours?' She's incredulous.

'It hopped up there.'

'It can fly.'

'I thought it was going to toddle under a car.'

He shakes his head at the water she's brought. 'It had a good drink. From the gutter.'

'Well – whatever happens now, it's better off there than in the chimney.'

She puts the bowl down in the front hall. She runs in to slip on her shoes and her cagoule from the coat hooks in the hallway. When she comes outdoors again he nods at her, still hugging himself tight with his Marigolds, then nods upwards. The gull is on the roof of the house opposite, partly hidden by the guttering. She runs down the steps. He walks back across the road to her. It's now raining, not hard, but quite steadily.

She shivers. 'It's amazing.' There's rain on her face.

'Come under the tree.'

Under the wet conkers and shining leaves, they shelter a little from the rain. New, fresh rain. Clean rain. They watch the bird.

She peers out from the tree. 'What's it doing?'

'It's cleaning itself. Sorting out its feathers. I think it's going to be alright.' He sighs, a huge lungful. 'I thought it was our sacrifice to the gods. Our payment for having such a nice honeymoon. Letting it die.'

She's never seen anything look less like it was going to die.

He's huddled in his cagoule, holiday flip-flops on bare feet, hugging the tablecloth round his shoulders. 'Imagine. If we'd left it there.'

She nods. 'I thought it was a pigeon.'

'I wish we'd done that forty-eight hours ago.'

'I didn't know we could.'

'A gull. Imagine if we'd let it die.' He shudders. 'Poor gull.'

New, fresh rain. She's trembling a little in the cold. She realizes she's still wearing her thin pyjamas. Her canvas shoes are getting wet through.

The gull's bathing in the rain, the guttering a birdbath. It stretches its wings twice, casting a flurry of raindrops as it fluffs its feathers. She thinks she can see the plumage whitening.

ON MARGATE SANDS

Angela and Lisa sit on the Harbour Arm, eating chips.

The sky looks like the fighting *Temeraire* ('except the sunset is in the wrong place,' says Angela). Lisa, who is used to south coast seaside, suddenly twigs that they are facing north. She gets out her camera, winds it on and takes a photo of her friend, orange hair against the orange sun. And then one holding up a wooden spoon of mushy peas. 'Guacamole,' says Angela to the camera.

They have been here a day. Dreamland has begun its decline, and the Turner gallery will not be built for twenty years. Margate, they agree, is a bit of a waste land.

It's Michaelmas term (although Angela and Lisa do not call it that), and it's not warm. The chips are delicious, wrapped in cornets of paper and soaked in vinegar. Lisa has ketchup on hers, which is 'just wrong', in Angela's opinion. They eat them all, especially the crunchy bits at the end, unwrapping the cornet to find them.

Lisa takes out a pack of Marlboro Lights, and they promise each other that they will give up once they have finished their dissertations. They huddle together over the flame and then pull their hoods up and scrunch their sleeves into their fists to smoke and watch the day come to an end.

As night falls they walk further into it, east along the esplanade, past the Winter Gardens and the old 1930s Lido, towards Cliftonville, where their B & B is. They dropped off their bags this morning.

At an off-licence along the way they stop and get cold beer. They smuggle it into the B & B, all net curtains, chintz and china and a curly 'Vacancies' sign.

They sit on the twin beds drinking lager from cans and looking at the newspaper and the tourist leaflets. The weather forecast is sunny tomorrow, and the clocks go back, which means they will have an extra hour. Angela wants to visit the shell house she remembers from day trips here as a child. Not the Shell Grotto – she looks at the picture and doesn't think they're the same thing. But they can't see any other reference to the shell house, so Lisa says they must be. Lisa wants to go on the Big Wheel.

They force themselves to do an hour's silent reading before bed, *Speech and Phenomena* for Angela, and *Gawain and the Green Knight* for Lisa, making it to forty-five minutes before Angela can't stand it any longer.

Angela talks vaguely about the Derrida essay she is writing. She thinks it will help to talk it through but it doesn't make sense when she tries. She wonders whether she could structure it using the lyrics of the Scritti Politti song, 'Jacques Derrida'. Lisa is doubtful. 'It's a good idea though, isn't it?' says Angela. Lisa grunts.

They make their way through Lisa's cigarettes, saving one each for the morning. They get an early night, which means eleven o'clock ('but really ten'), and are up at eight, coughing over the ashtray.

In the empty breakfast room, with its crowded tables and chairs, its artificial stems in vases, they fill themselves with eggs and bacon, toast and jam.

Angela is excited about her Derrida essay. 'I slept the best sleep I've slept for months,' she says. 'The Scritti Politti was a real breakthrough.'

'Pace yourself,' says Lisa. 'It's not even week four.'

'This is the best meal I've had in weeks,' says Angela. 'I really want a cigarette now though.'

'I saved a bit of mine,' says Lisa, ever provident, and they share half a chipped Marlboro Light over a refill of coffee.

'Perhaps we could go to a record shop in the afternoon,' says Angela.

This morning, at half past nine, fresh cigarettes lit, they climb down a metal staircase to the beach. They take off their trainers and socks and walk, single file, along the water's edge towards the Main Sands. Sunlight glances off the sea, the chalk cliffs still in shadow. They've packed day bags with towels and extra clothes and the tourist guides.

At a small cove just before they reach the Sands they sit down, spreading their towels a few yards from the sea. Apart from a couple of dog walkers, there's no one about. They can hear the quiet lapping of the waves.

'Clacton Pier,' says Angela, pointing. The day is unusually bright, the sun an hour higher in the sky than yesterday.

Lisa cracks open *Gawain* and lies on her stomach to read.

Towards midday they get up and head for the main beach, which is busier with day trippers.

'Let's go on the Big Wheel now, before we have lunch,' says Lisa.

They cross the road to Dreamland and stand in the queue. As the Wheel empties, it's filled again with the waiting people, winched up pair by pair to let the next carriage drop to the ground. Each carriage is a pendent lantern. Angela and Lisa step into theirs and are shut in with a clank of cold metal. The floor moves under their feet as the lantern stirs on its wire. It all feels madly unsafe.

'We should have got an ice cream,' says Angela.

'It's October. We're about to have our lunch.'

They watch the other passengers being loaded in, until they rise halfway up and can see over the fence and then right above the clock tower, whose bell begins to strike twelve as with a lurch they move up to the top.

Angela rattles the carriage. 'This is *very dangerous.*'

Both girls giggle hysterically. It feels suddenly windy, much more exposed than on the ground, even with a tin roof over them. Angela's hair streams, a flame in a hurricane lamp. As the clock's chimes ring out they look down at the fairground and wave, and then down through the bars at the carriage below, and across the town with its Regency and Deco and its wretched tower blocks, and across the Sands. Lisa takes a photo from every direction. Then they drop down and the people who were below them are now above them, at the top, and their view is of girders and spokes.

The wheel revolves smoothly. It clanks and creaks, but the sound is monotonous and restful. Many of the gondolas are unoccupied: they look like empty birdcages.

When the ride ends they are at the top, where they remain while the first carriages are unloaded, the cage doors opening and clanging shut before the wheel shifts round, and again and again until they are ushered out.

They go on the dodgems and waltzers and then have lunch in a caff – fried egg sandwiches and chips, with strong tea to follow. Angela wants to find 'Jacques Derrida', so they head into the shopping streets. In the flagstoned alleys of the old town they look at the curved-glass shopfronts, the dates in the masonry and the painted brickwork ads, and they browse the displays of junk shops and earmark the good-looking pubs for later. Lisa holds Angela's ice cream as Angela combs through the records on a market stall. It has some Scritti Politti but not that song. She gets directions to a second-hand place a few streets away. It's got a wire grille on the windows and black-painted walls. It's shut, but she rings the residential bell and the owner answers.

The stock is piled high and the man is knowledgeable, and finds Angela the record. Sipping a coffee and smoking a rollie, he lets her listen to it and she buys it. She leaves the shop triumphantly, brandishing the carrier bag, and he locks up again.

'I've got the words all going round my head now,' she says.

'Cashanova,' says Lisa. 'How you gonna work that in?'

Angela packs 'Jacques Derrida' carefully into her bag.

From the record shop they follow the signs to the Shell Grotto. They pass the Tudor House and take a quick detour into its grounds, making a plan to visit it properly before they leave in the morning.

'Is this where you remember it being?' says Lisa, as they walk up Dane Road.

Angela looks around her at the streets and houses. 'Maybe. Although I think it was less built up, more a quiet country lane.'

'Not much countryside around here though.'

As they approach the grotto, Angela says, 'I don't think this is it.'

'Let's go inside.' Lisa goes in.

'It didn't look like this,' says Angela. 'It had a garden.'

'Could it have been redeveloped?' says Lisa, coming out.

'I remember, very clearly, standing in the lane,' says Angela. 'My brother was leaning on the gatepost. I think we were waiting for my father.'

'Come on in.' Lisa pulls Angela in and pays for their tickets.
'We close at four,' the woman says.

'This isn't it,' says Angela, looking around the walls and shaking
her head. 'There are no shells here.'

'The shells are downstairs,' says the ticket attendant, smiling.

'Come on,' says Lisa, taking Angela's hand and pulling her
to the stairwell.

Its walls are black and caked with something that looks and
smells like slime. A very faint glow of lamps lights the narrow
steps. The girls descend the spiral staircase, Lisa leading and
Angela following, clutching the back of Lisa's hooded top.

The stuff on the walls is oxidized shells set into blackened
mortar. As they climb into the blackness the smell gets stronger –
damp and cold-dark-places and stagnation, with perhaps an
undernote of sulphur.

'Phosphorous,' says Lisa.

'This is a cave,' says Angela, as they emerge into the first
antechamber.

Low in the wall, recessed shelves sit like catacombs, or votive
alcoves. Electric sconces cast a dim light through the passageway.
Chambers loom out of the dark, studded with shells from floor to
ceiling in patterns of trees and flowers, stars and suns. The sharp
edges of mussel shells fan outwards.

Tracing their way around a circular channel, the girls edge past
a slightly plump child and his middle-aged parents.

'This definitely isn't it,' says Angela.

'But it's pretty cool, huh?' says Lisa, flicking on her lighter to
examine a wall.

They complete the loop and step into a cavern hall, complete
with altar.

'The place of sacrifice,' says Lisa, taking a photo.

The boy and his family enter the room.

'Crazy shit,' says Lisa.

The mother looks at them in annoyance.

'D'you think they get bats here, at night?' says Lisa.

Angela shrugs. 'How would they get in? This isn't it. Let's go.'

'Oh come on. It's fun.'

'It isn't fun. I didn't want this. I wanted to see the shell house.'

'You must have misremembered it.'

'I didn't! I didn't misremember it! I didn't imagine it.' Angela is starting to shout. The sound bounces off the walls.

'OK,' says Lisa. 'OK.'

'What are you looking at?' Angela shouts at the boy's parents. And then, at Lisa, 'I remember. I was there.'

'OK.'

'It was a little old lady's cottage. Every surface of the house and garden covered in shells, and garden gnomes made of shells. She'd done it all herself.'

'It sounds lovely.'

Angela starts to sniff. 'I bought a shell ornament there. An owl.'

'Do you still have it?' asks Lisa.

'No,' says Angela, with a sob. 'I don't have it any more.'

Another visitor enters, looks at the tableau, and leaves again quickly.

'We'll find the shell house,' says Lisa, patting Angela's back and trying not to look at the family. 'The woman on the desk will know.'

Upstairs the woman's eyes dart from Lisa to Angela, Angela to Lisa, Lisa to Angela. She doesn't know about a shell house. This is the Shell Grotto, the only one. Lisa thanks her and they go, Lisa pushing Angela out of the door.

Outside, she says, 'Are you sure it was Margate, Angela?'

'Yes it was Margate! I was in secondary school when I last came, in my first year. A girl from school came with us.'

'Would she remember?'

'We're not in touch.'

They walk back along Dane Road and into King Street.

'What about your family? They'd know.'

Angela looks up. 'My brother. He'd know.'

'Shall we call him?'

In a urine-smelling phone box on the seafront, Lisa holds the door open while Angela dials home, a stack of silver change on the ledge in front of her.

Her brother answers, but he doesn't remember.

'You were nine!' shouts Angela. 'You must remember. A whole house covered in shells, like the gingerbread house. An old lady made it.' And then, after a silence, 'Don't you remember, Michelle came with us in the car. You liked Michelle.'

Angela leans against the phone box wall, the metal frame digging in.

'Do you remember my owl made of shells? I used to keep it on the windowsill.'

Angela feeds the machine with silver as her brother talks. Through the panes of phone-box glass the sun is beginning to set. Lisa squeezes herself in. The urine smell blooms up as the door springs shut.

'I don't remember anything else,' says Angela to her brother. 'Just the house, and Michelle being there. It's all a blank.'

Angela is pressed into a corner of the booth, hunched over the receiver away from Lisa, her free hand over her face and in her hair.

Lisa looks outwards at the sunset distorted by glass. She lights a cigarette and, when Angela snaps her fingers, gives one to Angela too. The smell of smoke overtakes the smell of piss.

Over the Harbour Arm, the sky is darkening.

'Nothing,' says Angela. 'Nothing.' And then, 'No. I don't want to talk to her.'

She rings off and swipes at the stack of change, sending it flying, then bursts into tears.

Lisa crouches down and picks up the coins by their edges, holding her breath and trying not to touch the floor. She wraps them in a tissue.

'Let's get out,' she says, and pushes open the door.

Angela stumbles into the fresh air. 'Why doesn't he remember?'

'I suppose nine is quite young.'

'Where could it be?' sobs Angela. 'It must be somewhere.'

'Perhaps the old lady died,' says Lisa.

This just makes Angela cry even harder. She slams her bag against the phone box. It connects with a smash.

The two friends look at each other and Angela stops crying. Her hands shake as she kneels on the pavement and undoes her bag, pulling out the contents, cradling the shattered fragments of 'Jacques Derrida' as she tips them out of their paper sleeve and tries to piece them together on the street.

Lisa watches as Angela fits the pieces over and over again, a jigsaw or a mosaic.

★

The Tracey Emin show is great, but dense, and needs to be seen in stages. Lisa sits on the shoulder of the Harbour Arm where they ate their chips, where she took the photo. You can walk to the end now (the fingers?), which she doesn't remember being able to do (at least, she doesn't think they did). There's still a fish shop on the front, perhaps the same one, its queue snaking out of the doorway. Though tempted, Lisa has opted this time for an overpriced panino from the Turner café, and a decaf latte.

In the new tourist information office situated in the Droit House on the Arm (now adorned with an Emin neon), Lisa scours the brochures. At the counter she asks casually about the shell cottage. 'You mean the Shell Grotto,' says the woman, handing her a leaflet.

'I'm not sure,' says Lisa. 'I'm looking for something from the 1980s. A house covered in shells? A kind of folly – outsider art.'

'This is the one,' says the woman, pointing at the Shell Grotto picture. Lisa smiles and thanks her.

Wandering out of the Droit House, she happens upon Mark Wallinger's shed: the *Sinema Amnesia*. Unsure whether it's open, she crosses over, finds the doorway, and peers in. The elderly usherette beckons her and gestures the seat. Lisa sits down in the black box. In front of her, the fourth wall appears to be a fine metal scrim, through which the sea is visible. She looks out at the view for a while, and then around the black walls of the cinema booth: there is nothing else.

'I don't get it,' she says.

'It's yesterday's view.' The usherette hands her a flyer. 'You're watching what happened twenty-four hours ago.'

Lisa gets up and peers at the wall in front of her. It's not a scrim: it's a projection. She laughs. 'It looks exactly the same as today.'

The woman shrugs and smiles. 'Doesn't always,' she says.

Lisa gazes out at yesterday's sea and sky. They're blue, and calm, and full of sunshine.

THE CRÈCHE

Cursing Jessica and Mirosława, I pelt along the Commercial Road with my daughter in the sling, knees groaning at every jolt. At the crossing for the station we meet another mum, with a two-year-old in a buggy. I recognize the look of agitation more than the face, but I've seen her somewhere before.

'Just in time,' I say.

She nods. 'These lights are always slow.'

We make it to the island and then to the other side, articulated lorries menacing us with their engines.

We get to the station at ten on the dot. Jessica and Mirosława, in cagoules, stand at the centre of a small group.

Mirosława is looking faintly embarrassed, as well she might, and is holding a large white cardboard box, which is already lightly drizzle-spattered. Jessica clutches a clipboard and guards an enormous plastic crate by the station entrance. I know some of the other families: Sushmila and her mum, and a white couple I've met in the park with their newborn.

'Goo-ood morning,' says Mirosława, with that slightly twinkly, slightly world-weary way she has, that says *I have seen worse hardship than this.*

I take Jessica's clipboard, hold it at arm's length past my sling, run my finger down to find our names, tick the box to say I've paid, and sign the disclaimer.

'Does that cover land-based drowning?' I quip.

Jessica opens her crate. 'I've brought wellies,' she says. 'And waterproofs for everyone. What's Katie's size?'

'A five or six should do it.'

She hands me the wellies and a red all-in-one hooded waterproof, '18-24' emblazoned on the front in marker pen, with the Centre's initials.

I nod at Mirosława's box.

'Cakes,' she says with a quiet lift of her eyebrows. 'It's Ayo's birthday.'

'O-o-ohh.' I raise my head in greeting to Ayo's parents, both of them here today, standing slightly apart, smart in belted jeans and ironed shirts. They smile. His mum's got an oxygen canister on her back, attached by a long plastic tube to Ayo's nose, and his father pushes a holiday-sized suitcase. I smile at them and keep smiling as I let my gaze fall away.

'His first trip to the sea,' murmurs Mirosława.

'Here are your train tickets,' says Jessica. 'And this is just a little activity pack.'

The Ziploc bag contains a small satsuma, three cheap crayons, a sheet of paper and a green sand mould in the shape of a starfish. She'll like that.

Nancy, my Chinese friend, arrives, bumping her buggy up the stairs. She's not normally late.

I go to help her. 'You thought it would be cancelled?'

She laughs. 'I waited for a text. It's gonna piss with rain.'

87

'Never mind, I've got Factor 50 sunscreen in my bag. They can share it.'

Nancy signs the clipboard, pays the balance, and gets water-proofs, wellies and a blue seahorse for Ava.

She shows it to me. 'It's nice of them, right? They don't have to do this.'

'Yeah. It is.'

Mirosława comes over to us. 'We're still waiting for six families. But we don't want to miss the best of the day…'

Nancy catches my eye.

'… So we'll get on the train in one group now, and Jessica will wait for the others.'

'Righty-o.' I adjust my sling and heave my bag onto my shoulder.

'Can I carry something?' says Mirosława. It's the guilt.

'I'm alright,' I say. 'You look after those cakes.'

'Cakes?' says Nancy.

'It's little Ayo's birthday. The twenty-four-weeker.'

'O-o-ohh.' She turns to stare at them. 'Is that oxygen?'

'Must be.' I don't look round, and try to push ahead a bit so they don't hear us. But when we're all on the platform I stroll over and crouch down by the buggy to say happy birthday. I don't take his hand because I don't know where he is with infection control, although I presume he's alright if he's allowed on an outing.

As the train approaches, Mirosława shouts out that we'll all get in the last carriage. It's almost empty anyway. No one with any sense is going to the seaside, not today.

Nancy and I find two four-seats across the aisle from each other so we can spread out. I tip Katie out of the sling and set her up at the tiny side table with the crayons while I peel the satsuma and rummage in my bag for a bib to save her T-shirt.

Mirosława perches opposite me to take a photo of Katie and then one of Ava, also drawing, with the view behind her.

'I think we're going to be lucky with the weather,' she smiles.

As if in answer, a sound like gravel spatters the window next to me and runs down the glass.

I get out my ticket in case the inspector comes by, and stare at it, calculating how many bus rides to the city farm we could get for the price.

Nancy passes me popcorn and I pass her rice cakes, spreading them with Philadelphia from a plastic knife.

'Look, Katie!' I say, as fields enter my sightline. 'Sheep!' I reach over and lift her up to the window. 'We might even see some horses!' And we do, whole packs of them.

As the sky clears a bit and the rain dries up, the landscape changes to a silty grey, lined with tall chimneys and shipping containers: industrial Essex. We pass Pitsea and I kneel up on the seat for the first glimpse. I see Nancy slip Katie a biscuit while I'm not looking, huge diamond on her finger dazzling me as usual.

Then I spot it, in the distance. 'Katie, there it is!' I say. 'The sea! It's the sea!'

Mirosława comes back down the carriage and leans on the headrests repeating the same phrase. 'Just two more stops, so if you want to use the toilets, change nappies…'

We're coming into Leigh-on-Sea now. Weekends in my grandmother's caravan – but I haven't been here in years. I start humming an old TV ad jingle, to the tune of Dylan's 'Subterranean Homesick Blues' (though I found that out later): 'Ma in Marlow, JEAN IN HARLOW! Lee in Leigh-on-Sea, all saving merrily.' I watched that on my grandma's telly too, great big rented beast.

'Next stop,' says Nancy as we pass Leigh Marina, and I start gathering the things back into my bag. The window's filled with nothing but grey sea now: sea, and the occasional derelict warehouse. Boats in rows, hundreds of them, keels upward or tarpaulined over, lying yards from the track. An old seaside shelter, empty. I sweep a wet wipe over the table as a gesture at the crayon marks and scoop up the crumbs and the peel. I put it in Nancy's outstretched hand and she pops it in the bin. I slip on my sling, chuck Katie over my shoulder and wrestle her fat legs into it. 'Here we are,' yodels Mirosława down the carriage. Nancy stuffs Ava back into her buggy and we all pile off the train.

The station is an old-fashioned coastal one: whitewash, and iron girders painted battleship grey.

'You can see the beach from here,' says Mirosława. 'And it's not too cold!'

There's no lift, so we help with the buggies.

At the exit we turn right and file down a zigzag ramp to the beach – a long, thin, shingled stretch of shoreline punctuated by wooden breakers. There's nothing here, no tourism. Across the estuary from us, a power plant and a row of gas holders.

We pass a two-by-two crocodile of yellow-tabarded three-year-olds, also out on their end-of-year treat. They look like little ducklings, and they sound like them too. They each carry a bucket and spade.

'There's a shelter a bit further along,' says Mirosława, 'and some toilets. We'll camp ourselves near there. There's a drinks shack too, nearby, so we'll have everything we need.'

The shelter is round the back of the toilet block and itself looks like the proverbial brick privy, rotting benches running round inside in a horseshoe shape.

'We can leave the bags here,' she says. 'There's no one else around.'

We dress the babies in the waterproofs and wellies. With her hood up, Katie looks like a small spaceman. Nancy and I and Sushmila's mum lead our daughters up the ramp to the beach.

I shuffle off my plimsolls and peel back my jeans to mid-calf. It's like walking across a bed of nails, but the tide's in, so there's not far to go. I test one foot in the water: freezing. Katie waddles in with her wellies, eyes shining.

'Not too deep now. It'll get into your boots.'

'Toes!' says Katie.

'Really?' I take off her wellies and socks and roll up her leggings and waterproofs, wincing as she places her feet on the stones.

Sushmila's mum slips off her sandals and wades straight in, in her salwar kameez, sopping wet cloth clinging to her legs.

Mirosława approaches, smiling, and takes a picture. 'This part is a natural pool,' she says, tracing a rectangle marked out by poles. 'When the tide goes out it stays full of water. It really sparkles in the sunlight. Normally it's full of kids. Full of water wings and lilos.' She sighs. 'This area is always busy. You have to come early to get a good spot.'

We turn towards some noise and see Jessica and the latecomers, crunching down the beach towards us. The Chinese woman from Monday Rhyme Time and two families I haven't seen before.

'It's nearly twelve o'clock,' calls Jessica. 'I think we should eat our packed lunches before it rains.'

Mirosława nods and goes to help her with the picnic blanket. As they spread it, it whips up above their heads like a parachute. Jessica weights down one corner with stones but the wind blows them back in her face. Eventually they get all the corners and the middle ballasted with bags. Just then the first drops of rain start to fall, big and splashy. Katie and I stay put. The water's icy on my ankle bones. Ayo's mum determinedly paces the beach, oxygen bottle on her back, following Ayo as he crawls in front of her on the leash of his tube, trying to put stones in his mouth. The babies in their hooded waterproofs and wellies stagger over the shingle picking at seaweed, like so many tiny hazardous waste operatives. As the rain gets steadier, Jessica and Mirosława pull up the blanket and pack up, gesturing that they're going to the shelter.

The Rhyme Time woman speaks in Mandarin and Nancy laughs as she replies, then turns to me.

'I think we're gonna head into the town and get chips there. You coming?'

I shake my head. 'Don't think so. We've got our lunch.'

As the rain starts to power down on us we all struggle back into our shoes. Sushmila's mum wrings out her trousers. From further up the beach we see all the nursery children in their little tabards and shorts, rushing along with their buckets and spades and fishing nets on sticks, herded by bad-tempered teaching assistants. Our group's staked out the shelter, so I don't know where they'll go.

Some of the families have already found the drinks shack. The white woman I know from the park sits ensconced on the bench, hands wrapped round a hot coffee. Bet she'd like a fag to go with it but she won't light up in front of Mirosława. I grimace in sympathy.

The air is damp in the shelter. The bench is slightly damp too, so I spread out my sling to sit on. Soon we're all crowded in. The Chinese contingent has sloped off to find town, chips and tea, steaming up the hill with their buggies, rain covers on.

I unwrap our sandwiches from the clingfilm and pass one to Katie, wiping her hands as I do. Wish I'd brought a flask, I could murder a cup of tea.

The shelter is stuffed now, with people and prams, and their breath. Not everyone's got a seat, so they're just standing in the middle and the rain isn't letting up. One of the standing women pulls out a train timetable and her friend gets her things together.

As Katie and I crunch cucumber slices, Jessica moves through the shelter murmuring rumours of cake. She wades through the bags and buggies and makes her way to Ayo's family, who are sitting near me.

'Shall we do the cake now?' she says.

Ayo's father takes the white box off his lap and sets it down on the flat of the suitcase in front of him, like a coffee table. Ayo's mother holds him on her knees.

Jessica drags the coffee table out a little, to give it some room, then she stands on tiptoes and cups her mouth in her hands.

'We're doing cake now,' she calls out to everyone, swaying from side to side. She taps the shoulders of the people around her and gestures to the box, making a space around it. We all do the same, signalling and shushing each other in a ripple outwards. She brings the people in from outside the shelter.

Ayo's father opens the lid of the box and I gasp. Instead of doughnuts and pastries from the bakery, there is one huge square cake. I recognize the style – it's from the shop on the lane that makes them to order, and I realize it's not from Jessica and Mirosława but from Ayo's parents. The edges are piped in blue and the decoration is a cartoon tiger striped in black and orange. The words say 'Happy 2nd Birthday Ayomide'. The whole cake is banded with thick blue shiny ribbon in an enormous bow.

Jessica opens a carrier bag and passes out a knife, napkins and two candles in holders. Ayo's father pushes the candles into the soft icing.

'Let's sing "Happy Birthday",' says Jessica.

'Oh, let's light the candles,' I say. 'Someone'll have some matches...' I trail off, realizing no one will admit to it.

'The oxygen,' says Ayo's mum.

I blush and step back into the crowd.

We sing 'Happy Birthday' and then Ayo's father picks up the cake with the candles that can't be lit, and takes it round the shelter, picking his way over bags to show it to people who couldn't see.

Then he kneels down and unzips the suitcase and lets its lid fall back. It's full of party stuff: pink, blue, yellow, silver, gold and a foam of tissuey streamers. He pulls out handfuls of glossy party bags and starts handing them round, and packets of balloons, and gold paper crowns. Across the circle, Mirosława catches my eye and then begins to blow up a red balloon – three long puffs – ties it efficiently, hands it to a child, and takes another, stretching it between her fingers. I take a balloon and start blowing.

Ayo's father gives me a pink party bag, and a gold crown for Katie and one for me. We put them on. He takes out patterned paper plates and clear plastic cups.

Jessica brings back the cake and crouches down with it. A shame to cut it so soon, I think. Mirosława gets out her camera. Ayo's father and mother hesitate, but they take the knife in their two hands and put Ayo's hand over it too and smile for the photo as they push it down. Jessica tries to take the cake away but Ayo's mother holds onto it.

Ayo's father goes to the suitcase again and pulls out something else. I realize then that I'd heard them clink in the case and thought they were oxygen bottles.

He unscrews the caps, tearing the paper seals, pours drinks and passes them round. Pink lemonade, the fancy kind, in glass bottles like wine, with handwritten labels with raggedy edges, the kind made with real lemons.

Sipping it, I see the day they imagined for their child's first birthday party. Hot, July. A day like we had for ours. All the relations turned out, neighbours popping in, cake in the garden, rugs spread out, something fizzy chilling in a bucket. Everyone saying how well she looked, how she'd lost the baby weight. Cottony seedpods and sycamore drifting down on the breeze, the baby beautiful in a party gown. I taste champagne.

Except his birthday should have been November. Cold, blustery. Maybe a day like today. And of course she never had any baby weight, never had time. Ayo's mother sits with the cake on her knees, her arms linked round it.

I look in our party bag: a packet of biscuits, lollies, felt tips, holographic stickers, a balloon – I'll save that one for later. I look around me for more balloons and the hut is filling up with them, in children's hands and bobbing along on the floor. I pick one up for Katie, a yellow one. The rain's eased to a spit, so we go outside and play on the concreted area in front of the shelter. The balloon gets whisked under a hedge, so I rescue it. Katie bats it and kicks it in front of her. An older boy, maybe two and a half, tries to join in. Katie picks up the balloon and stalks off with it, clutching it to her chest.

Jessica is finally cutting the cake, scoring it into equal rectangles, leaving a quarter of it intact for the family to take home. The unlit candles lie by its side in their holders. I've kept the wax stubs of Katie's, white for the first one and yellow for the second, in separate pouches in the cutlery drawer.

Someone passes me a napkin-wrapped slice, and I taste it. Like wedding cake: that very thick icing, the firm, slightly stale sponge and the sweetened cream.

I see Ayo's father standing next to me.

'Thank you,' I say.

'It's for him,' he says.

I look at Ayo and he's smiling, the surgical tape wrinkling round his cheek. I think of Katie's presents at her first birthday party and I wish I had something to give him. We didn't buy any toys for a year.

I remember the starfish. I haven't shown it to Katie yet. She's still occupied with her balloon. I pull out the bag and unzip it.

I kneel down in front of Ayo and hold it out to him. He grabs it in a chubby fist.

'Dar,' he says, making the sign for 'Twinkle, Twinkle'. 'Dar.'

'I'm glad you like it, Ayo,' I say, and squeeze his hand.

Around me, people are doing up their coats and opening umbrellas.

'I think that's it for the good weather,' says Mirosława, turning down the corners of her mouth.

The woman next to me kicks the brake off her buggy and wheels it out of the shelter. I gather up our rubbish and put away our party bag and crowns. As people start to leave, Jessica darts through the shelter with a black bin liner, picking up napkins and bottles and squashed plastic cups.

Ayo's father wraps up the remaining cake and packs it carefully into the suitcase. He tries to give away some of the leftover party bags.

Mirosława looks at her timetable. 'Eight minutes to catch the next train,' she says.

Katie and I start to move. She's still clutching her balloon; the raindrops drum on it. I hang back and let her toddle but she's dawdling, and the others are far ahead of us, tearing up the zigzag slope to the station. They look like people on a helter-skelter. I pick her up and put her in the sling. As we pass a side path, the wind whips up her balloon and snatches it from her hands and she howls. I run down the path after it, chasing it as it bobs away from us before being whipped up into the air again and onto some gorse where it bursts instantly, the yellow rubber caught and flapping on the thorns. Katie's face erupts in red and she screams, as if she's going to burst too.

'Never mind, Katie,' I say. 'We've got another one. We can blow it up on the train.'

I break into a jog as we reach the zigzag, Katie bawling and arching her back all the way. Jessica trots up behind to overtake us, and Ayo's parents are a little way behind her, running with the suitcase and buggy.

'Her balloon popped,' I say to Jessica as she passes us.

Jessica makes a face of concern. 'I think I've got another one,' she says, feeling in her bag as she runs. 'I'll look on the train. And they'll have some more.' She points down to Ayo's family.

'We've got one,' I call after her. 'Katie, you can have a red one. We'll do it on the train.'

'Don't. Want. A red one,' screams Katie, and she cries as if her heart is broken.

I run halfway up the zigzag, ruining my knees – we weigh what we did when I was nine months pregnant – and then I feel Katie's foot digging into me and realize she hasn't got her wellies on. I call to Jessica up ahead and run back to look for them.

'It doesn't matter,' shouts Jessica, but it does. I skitter past Ayo's family to the bottom of the slope. Nothing there.

'Want the yellow one,' sobs Katie. 'Want the yellow one.' And I hold her to me tight.

Jessica looks down at me from the top and I wave her on. As I stop and lean forward to rest I see the others running out of sight into the station and then I see the train pulling into the platform, and then out again as I lean against the zigzag wall for breath.

We watch all the carriages with the people inside chug out west round the coast towards London, carrying everyone home. Katie likes trains.

Arms around her, I walk back along the shoreline towards the brick hut. I can't see anything on the beach, but I'd like to go back to the shelter, to check. The tide's going out now, exposing mudflats. There's the pool Mirosława talked about, peeling itself away from the sea.

LURVE

Vernissage: Look

Oh god, he's here, Jeanie is wailing. He's here, he's here, he's here.

Lottie feels a scrambling for her elbow, Jeanie dragging her over to the white-tiled wall of the old butcher's, into the cutting room.

Jeanie sinks onto a stainless-steel work surface. I can't see him, I just can't.

Lottie hoists herself up onto the counter. She takes a roll-up from her cigarette case and pats it down on the lid.

Jeanie is up again, pressing her forehead to the tiles of the wall, keening and swaying from side to side in her fur coat.

We're not staying in here all night, says Lottie, as she watches Jeanie roll her head against the tiles. They are artfully streaked with blood, Lottie notices. Or perhaps not artfully. Meat hooks dangle from an iron bar: it may be her imagination, but she thinks she sees bristles on them. Lottie lights the cigarette and smokes it.

This is *my patch*, says Jeanie. What's he playing at? What's he... (sobbing).

Lottie tunes it out.

Jeanie's perma-tangled hair has a slightly tacky gloss to it, of hairspray. Or something.

Are we all set then? says Lottie. Are we going in? Are we going to have a fag and pull ourselves together?

The crying subsides and Jeanie, still with her head pressed against the wall, gives something that could be construed as a nod. Or a convulsion.

Good. Lottie hops off the counter. She notices the sawdust on the floor, slightly bloodied: clev-er. (And is that a piece of offal? Some kind of entrail? *Very* good.) She turns Jeanie round by the shoulders, sticks a cigarette in her mouth and lights it.

Jeanie coughs. She wipes her nose with the back of her hand. Do I look alright?

She has snot on her cheekbones and mascara runs on the sides of both eyes. (And, when you look closely, telltale sores around the nostril.)

Yes.

Jeanie nods, and they leave the cutting room, just as someone else glances in.

How do you want to play this? says Lottie, drawing her friend into the main meat market, where the body of Look is installed.

Johann's head and shoulders can be seen across the room, navy fisherman's jumper rolled at the neck, arms folded, fair head nodding down at someone, unimpressed.

Jeanie turns round, keeping her back to Johann and fixing her eyes on Lottie's. I want him to see me first.

Lottie nods. So… let us get some drinks… and now lean down and listen closely to me as I pull you over here towards… *Time Out… Art Monthly…* Hackney massive… Deptford massive… Black man in a hat.

Black man in a hat.

Good choice.

They have spilled out onto the street, beyond Johann, to the smoking area. Lottie looks past Jeanie's shoulder. He's looking at you.

Jeanie flares her nostrils and waves her arms, splashing Lottie with beer and flaking burning ash onto her dress. She turns to Samson and laughs loudly at whatever he just said. And then she stares at him.

Can I try on your hat? she says.

Lottie levels her gaze at Johann. He meets it for half a second and looks away.

Shall we look at the art? says Lottie.

That's for amateurs. Let's look at the guest list. Jeanie picks up a clipboard abandoned by one of the girls on the door. She casts her eyes around the room.

Jeremy's here, says Lottie, tilting her head.

★

Jeanie is with Lottie, shamelessly scoping (he'll have to talk to her about that one day). She is wearing a fur coat that's slightly too big for her, and a leather pork pie hat. It's actually quite a good look. Ollie watches them for a while, Jeanie pointing people out to Lottie. They haven't seen him. He wonders if they've seen Johann – not that you can miss him, really. He takes a shot of them with the zoom. Then walks into the centre of the market and takes a few install shots, to get it over with. He gets another beer and walks over to them.

He strokes the coat. How many animals died for this?

I don't care. It's vintage. There's your blogger, Lottie – quick. Go and talk to him. See if he'll write a piece about Marcus, he likes you.

What are the key messages?

Doesn't matter – just go and chat him up.

Lottie grinds out her cigarette and scurries off in pursuit of the blogger. Jeanie continues to stare across the room.

He follows her line of sight over to Jeremy Deller. Are you still trying to shag Jeremy? He's not interested, you know. He thinks you're unhinged.

Did he tell you that?

No. But I can read people.

He is very attractive though, isn't he?

I suppose. If you were seventeen years older and starting to lose your teeth. Yeah, why not, why not?

Hello Jeanie. They look up. The accent is totally OTT, like something off a World War II channel. The height and the blondness also. Just – over-egged.

Jeanie stares. *Yo*-hann, she says. Her chin is trembling and her eyes start to fill. It is horrible to watch. Horrible.

Johann glances at Ollie and chooses to ignore him. He looks down at Jeanie, giving her his full attention.

It's nice to see you, he says (in that ridiculous accent). I haven't seen you around for a long time. (Cunt.) She doesn't say anything, just stares up at him, tearily. He nods at her. Anyway (he makes some kind of European face), I'm leaving here soon. Maybe I'll see you in the pub (he gives pub a weird intonation, like it's some kind of arcane slang). And he nods at her – nice to see you, he says again – and walks back to his group.

Ollie watches him go and then looks back at Jeanie. Let's key his car.

Jeanie nods. Yes, let's. She wipes her nose on her hand.

He rolls her another cigarette and lights it for her. He watches her face. Wanna see my etchings?

Silence. She is staring miserably after Johann.

How about my kittens?

Jeanie turns. Are there really kittens, Ollie?

Kittens. And Glenfiddich.

On their way out they pass Jeremy Deller, who looks at Jeanie's coat with, Ollie notes, some distaste.

The coat's a hit, says Ollie. You should wear it more often.

They liberate a couple of beers from the bar and swig them expansively along Whitechapel, weaving through groups of student nurses coming off shift, then cut through Stepney towards the piss-and-concrete of the Burdett Road, where both of them live.

They run the gauntlet of Bengali boys on the wall as they enter the stairwell to Ollie's flat, the boys – about twenty of them – quite obviously commentating in Sylheti.

It probably isn't complimentary, says Ollie, punching in the key code.

They'll set fire to a car later, says Jeanie.

Oh good, that's something to look forward to.

They hold their breath in the lift and pause on the walkway to take in some slightly fresher air.

Ollie opens the front door. There's a Britain First sticker on it that wasn't there before. He scratches at it with his key. So do you want a drink?

Where are the kittens? There are kittens, aren't there?

Course there are kittens. Would I lie to you about kittens? He pours them both a whisky.

Well, you are full of shit you know, Ollie. Cheers. She knocks her glass against his.

Ollie beckons her down the hall to his flatmate's old room. They're in here. He opens the door and turns on the small floor lamp, throwing a batik print over it to dim the light.

Ollie's cat lies on her side on a towel on the stripped mattress. She raises her head, lowers it again and closes her eyes. Ollie shuts the door carefully behind them. They sit on the floor by the bed. The three tiny kittens are nestled to the mother. The black one in the middle moves; the others are asleep.

Jeanie takes a cigarette out of her bag and Ollie shakes his head at her. Don't smoke in here, it's not good for them.

She puts the cigarette down in her lap. I did love Johann you know.

I know. But let's not talk about it now.

She gets up and reaches for something in her bag, holds up a small lump of hash wrapped in clingfilm. I'm gonna make this in the other room.

Ollie stands and follows her. He leans against the windows and watches her roll a one-skin joint.

They go out onto the balcony to smoke it, shaking with the cold and residual alcohol. They drape Jeanie's coat around their shoulders. Ollie shares out the DFs he gets from his mum and they wash these down with whisky. The Romanians next door are also on their balcony, in dressing gowns, similarly occupied: the woman gives a cheery wave. He pulls Jeanie to him under the coat as he takes the joint from her and draws on it. They watch a car burning out in the next street. He shuts his eyes and traces the crisscrossed scars on the underside of her arm. The DFs starting to work already, a numbness and a buzz at once, and he lays his head on her shoulder (he could fall, very far, very fast right now and he wouldn't care). That's the hum of the train on the Southend line. One Canada Square blinking red in the distance. A police siren, haunting and faint.

Ollie scans the roof terrace. Ad execs on the sunloungers and at the bar, glasses and bottles and pastel shirts reflecting the light. The blank blue glare of the empty pool – a dried leaf spins on its glassy surface. Dedicated afternoon drinkers – models, dancers, DJs – sit around its edge, already settled in. A girl in denim cut-offs and tights trails her hand back and forth in the water. Rufus Sewell dressed all in black. That other guy who nearly won an Oscar. Given the time of day, an awful lot of people.

He can't see the gallerist – or can't recognize him. He takes a deep breath, strolls the length of the terrace and makes another slow scan of the space. He looks out at the view, panoramic – cranes on the skyline and developers' hoardings below. Thirty St Mary Axe glinting green. The Oscar guy looks up and at him briefly. He starts to sweat a little, shifts the portfolio under his arm. He wouldn't mind a swim.

Finally, he sees him – squat, sixty, bald, wearing dark glasses. Lying like a Roman prefect on a sunlounger, cocktail in fat hand.

Ollie approaches him. The gallerist swings his legs over the side of the sunlounger, flips his glasses shut, tucks them into his shirt pocket, and proffers a hand. He is wearing workman's boots. Unusually, he has a Cockney accent, a real one. He sits with legs crossed at the ankles. He looks like a boiler repairman.

He gestures Ollie to sit down on the lounger opposite, and signals the waiter.

An attendant dips a net into the pool and catches the leaf.

★

Downstairs Jeanie and Lottie are trying to blag their way in. The front-of-house guy is stonewalling.

Jeanie sees Ollie emerge from the stairwell and peels herself off the counter. What did he say?

He told me to resist the siren song of easy, cheap success.

Well, you've resisted it thus far, says Lottie.

They walk past Trans Gallery twice before locating it, even though they've been there before: the lack of signage is always confusing. They try googling it and then remember it doesn't have a website, and doesn't appear on any maps. Jeanie has a number, but they won't be reduced to calling it. As they pass it the third time Lottie spots the entrance, replaced with an anti-squatter door now, for some reason, and half-hidden behind an industrial wheelie bin. They press the buzzer and are buzzed in without a word.

The room is silent, gloomy, empty. Ludmilla sits on a stool behind the counter. There may be some kind of acknowledgement of them, but it is too subtle and Slavic to decipher.

Ollie glances at the empty counter.

Nothing as gauche as a press release I suppose, Ludmilla?

Ludmilla spreads her ringed fingers.

A door swings open in the back to reveal a glimpse of the lurking Zsolt, and then closes again. The sound of a drill.

List of works? says Ollie.

She inclines her head.

Never mind. We can make an educated guess.

Ludmilla's eyes follow them around the room as they take in the show. After a few minutes Jeanie says, OK – I think we're done. Thanks, she says in Ludmilla's direction.

A fractional inclination of the head.

They step out into late sunlight. Not a bad show, says Ollie. I might actually review it.

Ludmilla would hate that. She'd never forgive you.

What would that look like, I wonder?

Magyars at three in the morning, says Jeanie. Long after you'd forgotten you'd upset her. She looks at her watch. Are we going to the Whitechapel PV?

That's Thursday.

This is the secret PV. Strictly guest list only.

Are we on the list?

No, but I can find out who's on the door.

They call into the Whitechapel Gallery and let Jeanie do her stuff with the reception and cloakroom. Ollie and Lottie sit on a bench in the lobby.

All set. Andriana's on at six. Let's get something to eat.

They instal themselves in the Hookah Lounge with mint tea and mezze until six, then wander back down the lane to camouflage into the first crowd, waved through by Andriana.

Ollie nods at the boys from Vinyl and gives a small salute hi. How come they were invited and we weren't?

Jeanie glances over the work. Made by the sort of people who think *Turps Banana* is cool.

Wait, *Turps Banana* isn't cool?

Do try and keep up, Lots.

Ooh look, says Ollie, it's a free bar.

Stationed in a corner, within strategic reach of the bar, they drink and look at the crowd, assessing who has been invited, who might not have been and why.

Lottie gets out her phone and begins to tap.

You make the notes in your head, Lottie, says Ollie.

I'm not making notes. I'm live-tweeting. She nods across the room. Who are those people?

Jeanie looks across. East End old guard. Robin Klassnik, Matt's Gallery. Cathy Lomax, Transition. Guy called Tim, ex-Vyner Street, now got his own thing in Peckham, keep meaning to look him up. Oh look, Jeremy's here. I thought he might be. I'll just go over and say hello.

Ollie follows at a distance and loiters a few feet away, looking at the work, as she greets Deller.

Deller looks at the lapel of her denim jacket. She is wearing a Fuck Art Let's Dance pin badge.

Wanna see my new tattoo, Jeremy?

No thanks. You're not allowed to smoke in here.

Rules are for fools.

A pause.

She takes the cigarette out of her mouth. What are you working on, Jeremy?

I'm thinking of making some kind of pond.

Cool.

Yeah. Maybe a few frogs, some newts. People could go pond-dipping. I need to think about it some more. I'd quite like to do another bat thing. Maybe in a belfry. I've been talking to Giles Fraser.

He's got a lot to answer for.

Yes, he has. So what did you think of the show?

Bit vacuous actually.

I did. I did too.

A flicker of interest.

So you gonna stick around here, Jeremy?

Think I'll go home.

Don't suppose you want to come back to mine for a cup of tea?

He shakes his head. No.

Line of something?

Goodnight Jeanie.

Jeanie turns around and meets Ollie's eyes.

Unhinged, mouths Ollie.

She turns away and studies a deconstructed painting.

Ollie walks over to her. Coming back to mine then?

No. You can come over if you like.

Gotta see to the cats.

Suit yourself.

Give me half an hour.

★

Ollie knocks on the kitchen light, chucks his keys on the table and fills the kettle. He picks up the post, glances through it and bins it. He takes the things out of the sink, re-runs the hot water and puts them back in again to soak, washing up a cup and spoon for tea. He checks the fridge and eats the last of the cheese, wandering into the hallway to look at the latest bubble-wrapped paintings lined up and ready to send. He'll have to sort a cab tomorrow, or a favour. He checks the bubble wrap once more, and the labelling, restacks them, looks in on the cat, rolls a cigarette, lights it, sits down at the kitchen table with tea.

He has a sudden thought and retrieves the Mac from the top of the wardrobe, sets it up on the floor in the hallway, out of sight of the windows, pops the memory card out of his work camera, slots it in and starts the download. While it runs he brushes his teeth and puts his toothbrush in his pocket. He lights another cigarette, scrolls past the work shots to the shots of Jeanie, saves them to a passworded folder on the hard drive and deletes them from the card. He deletes the work shots from the Mac.

Footsteps on the walkway – lots of them. A hissing sound: graffiti. Ollie gets up and goes towards the kitchen window.

Shadows falling across the frosted glass, and voices in Banglish outside. Then, distinctly: *Fuck off back to Shoreditch.*

The window shatters in front of his eyes.

★

Ollie sits in the kitchen of the woman two doors down as she cleans up his forehead. I wouldn't mind, he says, but I was actually born here. Y'know? I was born *up the road* from here.

Course you were, says the woman. They weren't, were they?

That's not what I meant, says Ollie.

Hold still, she says, peeling a plaster backing off with her teeth. Her earrings dance. There. All done. She surveys him and goes to the fridge.

Take this darling, she says, wrenching two cider cans out of a four-pack. Red lacquered nails and medallion rings on swollen fingers. She looks like his mum, in slightly better days. If his mum had ever seen better days.

Oh I couldn't.

Go on – you're in shock. She tips out some Craven A cigs and gives him a handful. Got a friend you can stay with tonight?

Shit. He remembers Jeanie. Yeah. Yeah I have.

The woman watches as he boards up the window (the slightly puzzling GO HOME scrawled beneath it in spray paint). Dunno why I'm bothering really.

I'll keep an ear out.

He checks on the cat, changes the litter and leaves out food and water. Wraps his cameras in sweaters and hides them behind the kickboard of the kitchen units. Slides the Mac back onto the top of the wardrobe. He takes his work camera with him in a battered bag.

Jeanie buzzes him in. The boys are on the wall, the same ones, or maybe their cousins. Watching, probably revelling. One of them is cradling a cricket bat. Ollie takes the stairs.

Jeanie opens the door. She is in her bathrobe, hair in a towel. What kept you? She sees his face. Oh shit.

Brick through the window, says Ollie.

Shit.

He hands her a can of cider and opens one himself.

Who fixed you up?

Woman down the way. He is gratified to see Jeanie look up, a bit too quickly. Bit young for me, he says, reassuringly. Can't be more than… twenty-five.

He sprawls in an armchair and starts to flick through a copy of *The Watchtower*.

Well, since you're here and dressed you can go to the Turkish shop.

I just got hit in the head with a brick, Jeanie. Alright. Alright. But I'm taking a knife with me, alright? He goes through to the kitchen and rummages through the cutlery drawer. If I get jumped on the way it's on you.

Get me a hundred duty-free, I don't care what sort, Silk Cut if they've got it. And a tenner of hash.

She hands him thirty-five quid. That should cover it. Tell them I sent you.

Ollie stops in his tracks and looks back at her. Sent me? *Sent* me?

Just go to the fucking shop, Ollie.

★

He looks up from the street and Jeanie, still with the towel round her head, is watching him from the walkway – he has guilted her into that at least.

He goes to the shop, powered by the knowledge of the knife and a wave of just-let-them-fucking-try-it adrenaline but he gets no trouble on the way (perhaps there is a warning in his eye).

He returns with the goods and is buzzed in. The front door is open: he closes it behind him.

Even the man in the shop felt sorry for me. He holds up the bag between thumb and forefinger and shakes it: This is more than a tenner.

Her hair is loose now, around her shoulders. He leans against the living room doorframe and watches her comb it with her fingers. She hangs her head downwards and blasts it with a dryer, then shakes it out again. A cigarette burns away in the ashtray.

Because it's not hard to drag me down, Jeanie. It's not hard. So there's no glory in it really.

★

Ollie wakes at half eight. He makes a cup of tea for himself and one for Jeanie, who's starting to stir.

She sits up and reaches down to the floor for the remnants of last night's bottle. Whisky?

Fuck it, go on then. He holds out his cup of tea and Jeanie pours it in.

He showers quickly and dresses.

Jeanie is now on the sofa in her dressing gown, cowering over a Bodum of coffee, a tower of ash on the cigarette in her fingers.

He takes one of her straights from the duty-free pack on the table, the warning in Turkish.

He stands looking at her for a moment. Are you going in to work?

She moves as if startled and the ash falls onto her hand. She's developed a bit of a head tremor lately. He wonders whether she knows, or whether to tell her. She touches her face, smearing it with ash. I'll go in later. I don't do my best work in the office.

Ollie checks his pockets. I should probably go in. Don't wanna get the sack. Not in winter.

Jeanie shrugs.

He takes an apple from the fruit bowl. It is mouldy. He puts it back and wipes his hand on his jeans. He picks up his camera, checks his pockets again. I'll see you later then?

Another shrug.

He lets himself out.

Finissage: Gentrification is nigh

Ollie knocks off work early and heads to the Whitechapel Library for the central heating, cheap snacks and comfortable chairs, the pleasantly bolshy staff, and the sense that all human life (except the artworld) is there. In Local History he lies down on a beanbag for a minute with his hands over his eyes, until a hijabi schoolgirl asks if she can get past.

He runs into Max Levitas in the upstairs café and gets him a cup of tea. Tell me about the whole thing all over again, Max, says Ollie, and the Cable Street veteran obliges.

Join the Young Communists, young man! shouts Max as Ollie leaves him.

I will do, Max, I will do, says Ollie.

It's the *only way* to defeat the fascists.

★

On the corner where Sweet and Spicy used to be, a Bengali working girl stands and smokes. The owner of the new restaurant bangs on the window to shoo her off. She bangs back and stays put. On the other side of the corner Jeanie is waiting for him, denim-jacketed, leaning with one foot planted against the wall like some kind of pastiche of a rent boy. She has taken to chewing

113

bubblegum. She looks utterly ridiculous. She pushes away from the wall as she sees him, and they fall into step.

Ollie shows her the email on his phone. Didn't get in, he says.

She takes it and reads, blowing a pink bubble, letting it pop and chewing again. That's brutal. She laughs and hands it back. What are you going to do?

Self-medicate.

Don't start without me.

When do I ever? He stops and puts a hand on her arm. Or do you just want to get hold of something and come back to mine?

Can't. People to see.

He lets go her arm and steps away slightly, increasing the distance between them as they walk on. She slows her pace to blow another bubble.

A small knot of people and some noise along Princelet Street catch their attention as they cross.

It's Georgie-Boy, says Ollie.

They watch along the road as a Muslim man high-fives George Galloway.

Apropos Georgie-Boy, says Jeanie, did I ever tell you—

Many times.

The Truman Brewery is already buzzing, the pavement crowded with people. Inside they find Lottie making notes on her phone.

Ollie nods at her tote bag. Another day, another stupid slogan.

Nice to see you too, Ollie. Did you get into the Open?

Thank you for reminding me. No.

Is that the third year now?

Fourth. Again, thank you.

Now, there are good pickings here, says Lottie. I just met someone from *The Telegraph* – off duty of course, but I got his number. I think that must be whatsisname. The hot new Pakistani painter.

Jeanie looks up. Hmm, he is quite hot.

People to see, remember? says Ollie.

He'll be a Muslim, says Lottie.

So?

So no alcohol, no sex. Sounds right up your street.

Jeanie smiles and strolls across the room.

Ollie shows Lottie the email. She reads it.

She couldn't curate her way out of a paper bag, says Ollie. That last show of hers was a pile of shit. Every single piece was a rip-off of something else. The hang was like a jumble sale.

Did you tell her that?

Of course I did.

You should set up a *salon des refusés*, says Lottie, with a smirk.

Ollie blinks at her. You did a gap year at the Sorbonne, didn't you Lottie?

Yes. How did you know that?

Lucky guess.

★

Jeanie approaches the Pakistani artist.

He looks at her. Hello. He is holding a bottle of beer.

You're Muslim?

Yes. He tilts the bottle and smiles slightly.

★

Who's that woman over there? says Ollie. One o'clock, in cobalt.

Lottie squints. It's Beth Serota. I've seen her picture in *Tatler*.

Do you actually read *Tatler*, Lottie?

It was in the dentist's waiting room.

Must be an upmarket dentist.

They drink their wine. Ollie regards Lottie. So when you were at school, he says, did you play hockey and lacrosse and that sort of thing?

Lottie gives him a withering look and returns her attention to the room.

No, I'm interested. Have you ever been foxhunting?

Lottie stares squarely ahead, blocking him out of her field of vision.

I watched someone eat a banana with a knife and fork once, says Ollie. It was fascinating, I couldn't tear my eyes away.

★

This is a Muslim majority area, says Usman.

Can't move for Muslims round here, says Jeanie.

But I'm the only Muslim in here.

Oh – Mustafa Hulusi's around somewhere.

Usman laughs. Under his arm, the latest issue of *BOMB*.

I haven't read that yet, says Jeanie.

★

What's Jeanie up to? says Ollie, looking round.

Lottie raises her eyebrows at him. He stares back, blinks twice.

She gestures across the room. Assimilating Islam.

They watch.

It's like watching the Crusades, says Lottie.

Shh, I'm trying to lip-read.

Can you do that?

It's my superpower.

As the Muslim artist looks the other way, Jeanie holds both hands up in their direction, and shakes a fist next to her ear.

She'll see us at the Ten Bells, says Ollie.

★

In the open doorway, Ollie puts a cigarette in his mouth and offers one to Lottie. Botoxed bitch, he says, aloud.

Oh, change the record Ollie.

He spits out his cigarette. What am I gonna do?

I don't know Ollie, maybe you should sleep with her. What the fuck are these, Ollie?

Craven A. I got given them.

Lottie wrinkles her nose. I see why you're trying to get rid.

Trouble is, says Ollie, when you're as good-looking as I am, people expect you to be talentless, to even things up a little. Maybe I should disfigure myself in some way, cut off an ear or something.

It's a good idea, says Lottie.

(He touches his chest pocket. The knife still there, days later: the shape of the handle through cloth.) I need to chuck a brick through a window, he says.

Shall we swing by the Ripper Museum?

Ollie glances back across the space at Jeanie, who is now talking to the Serota woman, apparently extorting her phone number. Yep, he says.

They wend their way back down Brick Lane. The touts don't even bother with them.

It's like they can't see us, says Ollie, as a gang of young Bengali men walks through them. They close the gap between them as they pass the men. Lottie's hair is shiny. Sharp.

We're the fair folk, she says.

★

On Cable Street, at the Ripper Museum, a suffragette is spray-painting a graffito onto the shutters. They approach and watch her work.

On fucking Cable Street, says Ollie. Fucking tossers.

Shall we help?

They drag over a couple of bin bags and rip them open in front of the door, spreading the detritus along the pavement.

The suffragette finishes her tract and nods a goodbye at them. She is about to conceal her spray can in her costume but instead holds it out to Lottie. Lottie takes it and the woman hurries back around the corner.

We need to get the pavement and road in too, says Ollie. The shutters will be open in the morning.

How d'you spell misogynist?

Not like that, but it doesn't matter.

Ollie picks up a builders' sign and hurls it against the shutters. An alarm sounds. They grab hands and fly round the corner.

When they've put some distance between themselves and the museum they slow to a trot. Ollie stops and lights a cigarette. How do you always look so sober, Lottie?

Because I am.

Oh. I was afraid it might be that.

They reach the Whitechapel Road. Lottie, he notices, is not walking with her usual briskness.

Are we going to the Ten Bells? he says suddenly.

She looks at him in surprise.

Cos we could... he looks at her. No, no – let's go to the Ten Bells. He takes a long drag of his cigarette, shakes something out of his head. They cross the road.

★

Back in its heyday, at the turn of the century, the Victorian pub was frequented by Hirst, Emin and Lucas. Now it's frequented by Ollie, Jeanie and Lottie. Half the private view is on the pavement, puffing at e-cigs through beards. As they step inside Ollie scans the crowd. There's Jeanie, at the front. With the Pakistani guy. From the look on his face, she is telling him the George Galloway anecdote. Yep, there we go.

He and Lottie fight their way to the bar and get a drink.

I've been hanging around this pub for four years now, shouts Ollie, above the din.

And has it brought you what you wanted? she shouts back.

Not really, no. He gestures to the back of the pub and they hack their way through. They settle next to a radiator.

He shakes his head and points to the ceiling. One of my works is hanging upstairs, you know. In a dark corner.

Lottie tries not to roll her eyes. Did you get paid in drink?

He looks at her, as though he knows she's taking the piss. And then he looks back towards the bar, where Jeanie is now sitting – *on* the bar – with the landlord of the Ten Bells and the hot new Muslim painter. The landlord looks quite taken with the painter (who is indeed quite hot).

Ollie is watching Jeanie, apparently transfixed. He sees Lottie looking at him and smiles, guardedly, and then looks back to the bar, to Jeanie and the Muslim guy. He shakes his head and mutters something under his breath. Now he is appraising the Muslim guy. Subtly – or so he thinks: he is slightly drunk (and is drinking quickly). But he is aware of Lottie watching him, glances back at her every so often, his eyes drifting across her face in something a little more than acknowledgement (yes, definitely drunk). And now he turns to her, he can't stand it any more, her looking at him. She watches his face, the planes of it. The contrasts. A few scratches still. The red mark on his forehead. He sees her looking at it and his hand moves to touch it. Healing up nicely, she says.

LAMMAS

The land shall not be sold for ever: for the land is mine

It wanted an hour of noon when we sallied forth down Marsh Lane. I carried a bunch of flowers as big as an ox's head, a companion furnished in like manner on either side. Taking up fallen twigs, willow wands, reeds and marsh horsetails, or our own walking aids, we perambulated the field, swishing at the long grass and Michaelmas daisies. Boys and women trudged along with picnic baskets and bushels of buns.

As we reached the first oak and tapped it with our sticks, I raised my flowers aloft. Now, this is not merely in fun that we do this, I shouted. When Comrade Barker and I are dead—

Which will be sooner than you think, said Ambrose, pointing his stick at the crowd. So prepare yourselves to step forward and take our places.

Thank you, Ambrose – you will know where the boundaries lie and if they are encroached upon. And you must do this too, and pass on the knowledge. Don't wait till they're grown up. They won't listen – will you, Kitty Edith? (That's my daughter there – a married woman now.) Take them round while they're small, like this one here, yes my dear, come forward. Like this one here. Would you like a posy? Aren't they pretty? Let's make you one from these daisies. This is your land, my dear. It belongs to you. And let no one ever tell you otherwise.

★

A crowbar had been produced. A heavy sledgehammer had been produced. There was a saw. Poker, tongs, pickaxe – people had brought all manner of things to take up the rails.

Where'd you get *that*?

I'm a blacksmith.

High railings were to be the object of our attack. Musgrave had climbed onto a table outside the Antelope that morning and told us the plan. If there were any arrests to be made, he said, they would have to arrest him first – and that they would not dare. We all laughed. He stuck his thumbs in his waistcoat and smiled from table to table.

On the marsh meadow behind the pub the fire brigade was holding its Bank Holiday fête, so there were hundreds of people watching us curiously. It was a stroke of genius to hold our meeting on Lammas and in full view of the fête entrance. The hundreds of revellers could not help seeing Musgrave on the table, clearly the ringleader, telling us the plan.

The brewers' horses and carts drew up, and the brewery men listened as they unloaded their barrels.

What if those fire engines though, said someone, what if they are in the pay, in the pay of the waterworks company? They have an endless supply of water. What if they are here not to have a fête but to turn their hoses on us? What if the fête is a cover for their real purpose? What then?

Musgrave said that he did not think that that was likely. But if they try to disperse us with a hose when we are but peacefully asserting our rights, then our lawyers will take up the case and make representations to the Crown. It will be a foolish fireman who tries to assault a Chartered Accountant and a Justice of the Peace.

And we all cheered again and hammered on the benches. Three cheers for Christopher Musgrave, I shouted, enunciating the name as clearly as I could.

Musgrave! Musgrave! came the chorus.

Now Musgrave made sure he was the first to lay his hands on the railings, in front of a crowd of witnesses including two JPs and our solicitor. With his hands holding the palings he addressed the crowd. We have given them notice to remove their property from our land, he said, and that they have failed to do. Therefore, we do it for them. With that, he pulled at the railings, to the accompaniment of loud cheers. The crowd surged forward and the fence came down. We went across the marshes to take up the track.

I took hold of a fire-iron and tried to prise away part of the railway. The hardest physical work I'd done was to dig potatoes in my own garden, and this became swiftly apparent to all who observed me. I wiped the sweat from my brow with my shirt. A few others joined my section of the track, and we managed to damage it sufficiently as to render it unusable, bashing it with shovels to warp the metal. It was satisfying work.

Musgrave had said at the pub that there was to be no wanton destruction of property, but this was not wanton, I reasoned. There was no other way to get up the rails.

Musgrave was pleased with the job. We have done what we came to do, he said – and the crowd roared – and we have done it with as little injury as possible. They carried him away, shoulder-high.

*

I helped Kitty to a boiled egg while Alice nursed the baby. I glanced at the clock on the mantel.

Get on with you, then, Edward. She'll manage on her own if she's hungry enough. Give her a piece of bread to chew until I'm finished.

I tidied the plates away hurriedly, made my goodnight kisses and took my hat, coat and shovel.

When I arrived, near six o'clock, they had torn down the fences and were deep in politics. About thirty were gathered on the green with sacks of tools. Ambrose Barker, the young assistant schoolmaster, was in full flow.

Keir Hardie's playing a bold game to get a name. The only one not an office-hunter is John Burns.

He had his jacket off and a pitchfork slung over his shoulder. I remembered then that he had been a farm boy, from Northamptonshire.

Some sheep came over to look at us. I sat on a sleeper – the new tracks looked dishearteningly secure and invulnerable – and took out my notebook and pencil. After a while I hailed Ambrose Barker and he took a seat beside me.

I'm going to write to the papers again, Mr Barker, about the library. Will you help me compose the letter?

Gladly. What has happened this time?

Nothing. That's the point.

Then we must find something relevant to mention. Can you complain about the composition of the committee? Or the slow progress of the meetings? Can you remind us how long it has been since the idea was mooted?

Wait a minute. Sirs – it is now two years since a public library was agreed for Leyton.

Good.

And we are no nearer a resolution. At the committee meeting last Wednesday night…

That's it. A brief, specific complaint, followed by a reiteration of the public good that will ensue from the establishment of the library. End with a vision from the glorious future and a wish to see it enacted here in Leyton.

Do you think it will be enacted here in Leyton, Mr Barker – the glorious future?

There's no doubt in my mind, Mr Pittam. It's just a question of which comes first – the library, or the revolution. But look now. Here come the reinforcements from Hackney. There's work to do.

He picked up a mallet and threw it from one hand to the other with a grin.

I put away my notebook, swung the shovel over my head and brought it down on a rail.

*

No sooner had the waterworks men relaid the track than our men arrived to undo it again. Charles the blacksmith led the charge. He was the size of two men and the heft of three. Once more the enclosures were uprooted and thrown down.

Somebody had brought torches in a leather toolbag, and the tarry smell as he lit them filled the air. Soon they were blazing all around, showing that we would not be moved and meant to work all night if need be.

An old white-bearded gentleman had come from Stratford to swell our ranks. High over his head, affixed to a walking stick, he carried a card on which was pasted a verse from Leviticus. He was brushed aside by a policeman, as a troop of them arrived to break up the gathering.

We had agreed that half a dozen of us, sacrificial lambs, would give our names and addresses, but the crowd had other ideas.

Don't give names! Let 'em find out, and let the company do its own dirty work.

Why isn't the leader here?

Oh, it's what they all do. Clear off at the first sign of trouble.

Our Mr Musgrave has shown the white feather.

Our Mr Musgrave? You think so? I don't trust these toffs.

Reckon he's a turncoat?

Turncoat, or a police agent.

Gentlemen, gentlemen, if you please! (I feared a riot – a disorderly one, where an orderly one was wanted.) Gentlemen! Listen to me. I climbed onto a wheelbarrow, my arms spread wide. You must understand what an injunction is. Mr Musgrave is forbidden by law to attend this site. He will go to prison if he breaks that injunction.

Oh, but he'll let us go to prison in his stead. I know that sort.

Gentlemen, please. I have here some letters – let me read them. It's all right, Inspector, this is a peaceful meeting. Gentlemen, Mr Musgrave is on our side. He is your best ally in this – but he must act within the law. We all must, or we are lost.

(I suddenly became aware of a smell of manure, and I wondered what the wheelbarrow had been used for.)

And this is within the law, is it? Laying rails on our land.

It is our land, and they are trespassing on it.

It is our land, and they shall not take it.

Let me read the letters – please.

No injunction against us, though, is there?

Please – let me read to you what Mr Musgrave has to say.

There was quiet for a moment, and I read aloud the letters – one from the waterworks company and one from Musgrave, which he had asked me to convey to the commoners by way of explanation for his absence. Barker hurried over and said a few words to me. I put my hands up again.

I propose that we adjourn the meeting for a week, I said – to ascertain if the waterworks company will comply with our wishes and enter into an arrangement such as we have put forward.

It was apparent that there was no seconder. But another gentleman, Alstrom by name, stepped up.

From what I can gather, he said, the land belongs to the people. (Loud cheers at this.)

… And the water company has taken it upon itself to lay down the rails. Until the company has obtained an injunction against us – against all of us, every one – we commoners ought not to hesitate to maintain our rights.

More cheering followed this.

A committee man, Mr Beadle, then counselled delay in case further writs were served, but was met with cries of No!

I tried again. I submitted a motion that we adjourn the meeting. Only two or three hands were held up for it, while the large majority voted against (though a number of people didn't hold up their hands at all).

The big fellow, the blacksmith, stepped forward with: Come along, lads.

This was all they wanted. Some dozen others followed his example, and they commenced scraping away the ballast from the sleepers, which were firmly embedded. Inspector Wallace rode up to them.

I see you're the ringleader. If there's a riot then it's you will go to prison.

No riot. We only mean to have our rights.

And he continued the work he had begun. Sacks of tools were

emptied onto the ground and men from the crowd grabbed at them. Torches blazed and were passed from hand to hand.

I jumped from my barrow. Very well, gentlemen. Then I leave you to do as you please.

The blacksmith nodded at me, and began to sing, and others took up the melody:

> *Work, boys, work and be contented*
> *As long as you've enough to buy a meal*
> *A man, you may rely, will be wealthy by-and-by*
> *If he'll only put his shoulder to the wheel!*

As I turned to leave, to the music of singing and hammer blows, a sergeant accosted me and demanded my name and address, which I refused to give. I am perfectly well known, I told him, and you know where to find me at any time. I am not going to facilitate the service of writs.

★

Ambrose let himself in, through the back door. He glanced at the page I was working on at the kitchen table – the pencil sketch and text.

A monument? he scoffed. Vanity.

No, not vanity, I said. Insurance. I turned it round so he could see. A nice solid list of what they tried to do, how we fixed it, and the promises we extracted from them in law. With dates and references. All in the hardest, most durable stone, picked out in gold and sited prominently.

Paid for by the word?

I shall work on it, I said. Like a telegram. And I drew the notebook back and licked my pencil.

Ambrose lifted the lid of the teapot and peered at the dregs within. I gestured to the clean cups and he took one and filled it.

He was a decent fellow, Musgrave, I said. He was well-to-do – he had a professional standing. And property, plenty of it. Didn't have to throw his lot in with us. What was it to him whether the commoners kept their land?

Top-hat agitator, in other words. A faint smile spread over Ambrose's features. He was all right. And he liked his name in the papers and a bit of notoriety.

★

Ella came with us to pace the boundary in advance of the ceremony, checking that we remembered it and that all was well. I didn't entirely approve of their set-up (and privately I thought Ella a snooty sort of Communist), but Ambrose was nothing if not consistent. We traipsed in silence.

I looked back over the field and remembered those August evenings of the nineties. Police horses and pickaxes and failing light. Myself a young man of nine-and-twenty, with a wife and three children.

I stopped. It was brave of us, was it not? I said, and they laughed. Our courage was eclipsed by the next generation's – we all knew that. But at the time, on our own no-man's-land, dismantling by night what was done by day, and at the end of our own day's work, with no sense of how long the game might continue…

Perhaps it was not particularly brave, I assented – and they laughed again.

Ambrose had had only himself to think of, as he always had. And Ella wasn't there, in those days. She didn't know what it was like.

★

I rapped on the gate of the stonemason's yard and pushed it open.

I called in earlier in the week.

Mr Pittam. Come in.

The mason sat down on an unfinished capital and perused the draft inscription. Ah yes, Mr Musgrave. Sir Christopher, I should say. I did his headstone a few weeks back. A sad loss. A nice commemoration, this.

That's what I thought.

Gold leaf?

If – that is to say – it is to be funded by the ratepayers, as the inscription says.

I have the list of charges here, in this ledger. He took up his chisel and turned it over in his hands.

★

We spread the cloths out on the field.

This is a good spot. Nice and visible. Make sure the banner can be seen from the lane, George.

Some young people arrived then, to join us on their dinner hour. One of them offered round Woodbines from a tuppenny packet. Alice and Kitty unpacked the hamper we had brought – watercress sandwiches, hard-boiled eggs, barley water, and the radishes, tomatoes and raspberries from our garden. Ella unwrapped meat pies and began to cut them up, handing round the pieces (careful, Ella – we've got some vegetarians). There were pears and greengages, from the vicarage orchard (I didn't mention their provenance).

Betty Edkins played the tin whistle, and the Solomon children entertained us with a display of toe dancing.

A young lad flung himself down on the grass beside Ambrose and me.

What do you think of them, Mr Barker? The new Labour men in government?

Oh, don't ask him that, lad. You'll be here all day.

Five-hundred-pound-a-year men all. Doing the Tories' work for them. Come to the Working Men's Club and meet the Walthamstow Anarchists. We're teetotal there, but you can have a game of billiards.

What do you think of Hitler?

Now listen. Today is International Red Day. Before we think of fighting Germany and Italy we must fight Capitalism.

Isn't Hitler fighting Capitalism too?

★

Could I have a pie, Mama?

Shh, they'll give them round. If I get a piece you'll have mine.

★

Did you go to Trafalgar Square in the spring, to hear the hunger marchers?

I did. I heard Tom Mann give his speech.

Do you think Labour will give it them? Thirty shillings a week?

MacDonald and his cronies! Do you think they're Socialist, any of them? Ha! They impugn the name of Socialism. Invertebrates, all of them. Spineless and gutless.

★

Have another sandwich, Sid, you're looking thin. Did you go and see my brother-in-law?

I did, Mrs Hagger, and thank you. He says he'll find me a day or two at the end of the month but he's got nothing regular. I've the loan of a bike next week, thought I'd go round the farms.

If I hear of anything I'll tell you. Would you take shop work?

I would, but I'm not much good at adding up. I can weigh things and wrap things and wash down tables and that.

*

Edward, I didn't tell you this morning's good news. I had a cheque in the post for a hundred dollars – no, don't get excited, it's for the League Against Imperialism, for our work on Meerut. The news has reached our American comrades, and they have rallied round.

Dilli Chalo!

Indeed.

Enormously kind of them. How will you spend it?

Legal fees. Food parcels. Bribes. We can arrange those things quite cheaply by wiring to India. I'm going to spend a very little on some simple pamphlets and stamps to spread enlightenment here. I was thinking of sending a delegation to the TUC.

TUC won't listen.

Maybe not, but it won't cost much to try. I thought I might try to meet Ellen Wilkinson.

I know Ellen Wilkinson—

You don't.

Well no, but I know her views, and she won't be interested in something so remote and unwinnable. Listen, Ambrose, there are three Englishmen amongst the prisoners. Focus on the Englishmen – no, listen. No one cares about the Indians. It pains me to say it, but it's the truth. Concentrate your campaign on bringing the English home. Appeal to their chauvinism – you'll find it in abundance.

*

Were you here in ninety-two?

I thought I recognized you. How d'you do? I'm Philip.

Fred. I was a drayman then.

That's right. You formed a union.

Much good it did us. Still – worth making a stand.

Did you find something else?

Eventually, with the drysalter's in Bermondsey. I live over that way now. Not everyone was so lucky.

★

The opiate of the masses – think about it. Doesn't have to be religion. Any opiate will do. What are the opiates round here?

★

Do you remember the blacksmith?

Who could forget him? He was like Hercules.

Hephaestus, you mean.

Both.

Well, he's alive, you know, and living in Rochford – nearly ninety and fit as a fiddle! Takes a turn around the village every day. I think he'll make a century.

I was never afraid of anything, so long as I was stood behind him. Always made sure I was.

Do you remember his roar?

And the way he looked at the horses – like he could mesmerize them at a stroke. I believe he could.

He was the size of ten men. And his strength!

I never saw anything like it.

★

Seen any good films lately, Councillor Pittam?

Oh I have, lad. Yes I have. I saw *Blackmail* the other day.

Did you really?

Went up to town to see it.

Is it worth seeing? I've a half day Saturday.

Here's ninepence. Buy yourself a ticket.

★

Mrs Barker—

I am not Mrs Barker. We are not married. You may call me Ella, or Comrade.

Comrade Ella, did you vote in the elections?

No, but I'm glad that those who wanted to were able to.

My sisters and I all turned out for Mr Brockway, and my mother too. I think he's going to be a great support in Parliament.

★

Well, Pittam here's a Liberal still. It's not that he hasn't seen the light, he just prefers to wear dark glasses, like those movie stars he's so fond of.

I'm not persuaded that the Labour group has the might to stand up to the Tories – no, not even in government. And I'm too old to wait for the revolution.

I think of him as a Liberal Communist.

★

No, I live in Sussex now, but I've come up today to visit. It was an occasion for Dad, you know. He tells the stories as though we remember it all, but my brother and I don't remember any of it, and my sister was a babe in arms. I do remember his campaigning for the library, later on. Now that was a useful thing. But my nephews use the lands for their sport and games, so

133

Dad has seen his grandchildren benefit. And the people round about, of course.

★

Somebody suggested to me the other day that the Boy Scouts—

Terrible pseudo-military organization. Filling young heads with dangerous nonsense.

Yes, but hear me out, Ambrose. This lady suggested that the Boy Scouts might fetch and deliver books from the public library to the bedridden. It's quite a good suggestion, I think. If they can't come to the library, then the library shall come to them.

★

I felt very important, carrying the slip to the ballot box.

★

I don't know that it was worth all Dad put into it, to tell you the truth. All those years of letters and protests. He could have done something for himself instead – for us – in the time it took. Mum would have preferred that, I think. I would have preferred it.

★

I think the money will be in talkies, in the future. Think of the possibilities.

Think of the propaganda!

★

But there weren't the opportunities then, for a man of his class. Still aren't, are there? Or he'd have been a solicitor, not a solicitor's clerk.

★

I'm talking about Utopia!

★

Do you like going to the pictures, Aggie?

I do, but my sisters don't, not much, and my friend that I work with can't afford it much. I'd go more often if I had someone else to go with.

★

Mother was a suffragist, and I did what I could, when I could spare the time from raising my children – they're nearly grown now. It is nice to see it come right in the end. Mother didn't live to see that.

★

There's no secret to the law, no mystery. All it is, is writing things down that have been agreed upon. And then knowing where to look them up later – that's important. And applying the rules. That's all it is. I did most of the solicitors' work for them, and I was in court every week. That's why I had no fear of the courts.

★

Of course he gets a small stipend now, as a councillor. Should have been a Member of Parliament, not a councillor.

★

I have a volume of Tacitus at home, Mrs Hagger, with the translation on alternate pages. Your son is welcome to it. No, not at all, I never open it. Tell me your address.

★

Maybe we could go to the pictures together one day, if there's something you might like to see? I could call for you after work one Saturday.

★

Yes, it's been a long day already. I came up first thing in the morning on the train and I go back this evening. But it's good to see everyone. It's getting harder now.

★

There is a Carnegie library at Lea Bridge, covenanted as a library evermore. There are commons here, where there would have been enclosed and private land. Walkways and bridle paths maintained. School boards better than they were. I am content.

That's your trouble, that is – contentment.

You're a bachelor, Ambrose. I'm a grandfather.

★

A gang of us took hold of the railings and we heaved and we heaved like a tug o' war and on the third or fourth heave they came away, and Bill here fell into the barbed wire. Still got the scars, ain't you, Bill?

★

Parliamentary Socialism is a contradiction in terms.

★

Dad. Dad! Oh, he's miles away.

★

What we need to talk about is the moral turpitude of Capitalism.

Here, Peggy. You can help me hand round the buns.

★

On your way, Musgrave. I thought it was you. You're the only one who'd come here dressed in a white tie and top hat. Oh, is that Humphreys there with you too? I thank you for your sense of occasion, but it's time for you to go now. We've got half the Secularist Society here. Don't want to shake their conviction now, do we?

★

My father was a Chartist, back home in Northamptonshire. He thought Parliamentary democracy would solve it. But where are we now? No further.

★

Back went the lines. Back went we.

★

The Nazi party is holding its rally today in Nuremberg. They say tens of thousands will march.

★

I was always at home on my own with three or four children while Edward was out agitating for a library or writing minutes for the ratepayers or whatnot. So I saw none of it.

★

All true Socialism is international.

★

Edward was quite confident he wouldn't go to prison. If he had, I would have killed him.

★

Morris was rich, yes, but he wasn't in it for entertainment or personal glory. He believed in the League. Worked harder for Socialism than anyone else I knew – and I knew them all, in those days. Oh look, oh look! Comrades! I see the gentlemen of the press approaching! It is time!

★

The silver band came up the lane, playing a marching tune, and we all followed in procession towards the manor building. Presently, the Mayor arrived with some of the aldermen.

Ah, just in time to get his name in the papers.

Hush, Ambrose.

Oh, I was forgetting. These are your cronies now. I shall become obsequious. Take your coat, sir? Whose bag may I carry?

While the band played, the Mayor, the aldermen and the newspapermen arrayed themselves before the manor house, ready for the unveiling.

Newsprint has its uses, Ambrose, but stone is stone. Think of it like a barricade. Should hold them back another thirty-seven years, don't you think? Look at all these witnesses.

As I swept my hand round, I caught sight of an old enemy, lately of the water board, also in attendance. His black hat and the scowl beneath it. Here to watch us lay the stone. What had he come for? Spectre at the feast.

The Mayor took presidence of the ceremony. After a speech of welcome, and of praise for the band, he called me forward, and I ascended the steps to the platform. I related the history of

138

the Lammas Lands, from King Alfred's time to now, and how on Lammas Day in 1892 the people of Leyton went on to the marshes and pulled away the fencing and the metals.

With that, I pulled the cord and unveiled the tablet. A cheer rose up and the trumpets sounded in triumph. I waved to the crowd and quickly climbed down again and retook my place. The people clapped and cheered again, and once more the Mayor gave a speech, full of nods to the pressmen.

The Deputy Mayor took the floor and proposed a vote of thanks to the Mayor, for playing such a prominent part in the decision to commemorate the acquisition of the lands.

Ambrose coughed loudly and prolongedly. My apologies, my apologies, merely the wheezing of an old man. Do go on.

Acquisition, I muttered. Defence.

Kingaby stepped forward then to second the vote of thanks, remarking in passing that had it not been for the ratepayers' association, the Mayor might never have taken such a keen interest in the commoners' rights.

Ambrose nudged me and pointed at the inscription. They've forgotten the apostrophe.

Both apostrophes, I said. There should be two. Do you think anyone will notice?

No.

I exhaled heavily. Will the young people carry on our work, do you think?

One never knows. It's all an act of faith, isn't it? Ironically. Perhaps they'll come up with something of their own that we haven't had the wit to think of yet.

The Mayor concluded his speech accepting the thanks, nodded to the bandleader, who struck up a formal air, and looked to me. I picked the flowers up and laid them on the platform against the building in front of the stone, as at a war memorial. Everyone followed my lead – the willow wands too, and the sticks and reed grasses. The child laid down her posy.

And then we left, repairing to the Hare and Hounds. Kitty took my arm, folding a gloved hand round it. This used to be fields too, I said, pointing to the buildings on the westerly edge. These were Lammas Lands too. But they were dislammased and sold off, before Ambrose and I were born.

SAMHAIN

There is smoke in the air. It comes from the gardens that back on to the park, hovering in blue wisps over the wooden fences. If they go closer they will hear the crackling, see the sparks: the collapsing, glowing matter.

It's starting to be sunset as they leave the toddler area and turn into the avenue banked on either side by playing fields. The park-keeper, wearing his woollen hat and donkey jacket, opens the casement noticeboard and turns the hands of the cardboard clock that says THIS PARK CLOSES AT. He turns them to five.

They have not brought the scooter today, so they walk, very slowly, holding hands. At the fields Danny, a younger park-keeper, stops his John Deere tractor (which they always admire), dried leaves piled in the back. He's made a jack o' lantern at the community centre. He's proud of it; he shows it them – bright orange to match his hi-vis uniform. They show him theirs. Wow, that's really something, I like the eyes. Yes, he's got a baby now – his wife had the baby last month, it's six weeks old: Devonie. Pretty name. And so lucky to be September-born, for school, you know. Lovely time of year. Welcome to the club. He waves, drives off.

Under the trees. Most of the leaves on the grass now, playing fields golden in the low sun, shiny red jewels catching the light. A late conker found today, maybe the last of the year, but fresh, gleaming – the white top vernixy, dissolving when she rubbed it with her thumb, the burnish almost damp. She feels it, round in her pocket. Waits while her child inspects a tree trunk, mossy on the north side.

The lost mitten balanced on the sapling, where it's been for a week, getting rained on, frosted, thawing out – she unhooks it, slips it in the plastic bag with the lantern and the other things. No one will miss it now.

Past the logs – wooden structures, stumps and trunks for children to play on, sunk here at great expense by the council a year or so ago, shortly after they moved in. Getting nicely weathered, in that silvery-grey way wood does. Part of the landscape.

A horse chestnut leaf on the path, huge and dried and umbrella-like. Blight-patterned. And the leaflets curl inwards like elves' slippers. She shakes it as they walk, rattling them home.

At the park gates she stops for her child to catch up, so they can leave together and cross the road, holding hands, quickly and carefully always, looking both ways even though it's a one-way street, not all the drivers know that.

Down their road, towards the shop at the end, to buy apples, watching, as they slowly progress, the first pumpkins being put out. A butternut squash dressed as a witch in a frayed black cape and hat, face drawn in black marker, twigs for arms, sitting on a doorstep; a pumpkin, not yet lit, in the window of an upstairs flat. A woman dressing the privet hedge rather generously with nylon cobweb – she turns and flashes a smile. Past their own flat – glittery bats in the window, cut from black sugar paper. How the shift of sunlight on glitter catches the eye. The rowan tree outside heavy with berries.

A man across the road comes out of his front door with two large pumpkins in his hands, places them on the sills and strikes a match. You can almost smell it.

A small, early group of trick-or-treaters passes by – preschoolers with painted faces and shiny costumes carrying little buckets or baskets, accompanied by a woman her own age, in civvies.

She peers at their faces, through the dress-up and paint. (Though how would an extra one slip itself into a group like that, counted and recounted every few yards?)

They cross at the lights. The greengrocer's fruit and veg display juts out like an apron stage. Shiny apples – red ones, green ones, Snow White half-and-half ones – every fifth one wrapped in pale violet. She could write a message on the paper, or a spell – rewrap it with the message inwards, tissue sealed with wax. She fills brown bags with the hard fruit, heaps them into a wire basket and pays at the till with crisp notes. On the counter toffee apples glisten in cellophane – she hadn't thought of those.

Laden with the bags she walks along the parade to the church and steps inside. It is dark and empty, lit by electric pillar lights and smelling of furniture polish. She makes some sort of vestigial, half-involuntary genuflection and crosses via one of the pews to where the votive candles blaze. An old man sits in the side chapel, coat and scarf on, hat in his hands. He raises his head and nods. He looks cold.

She selects a candle – white paraffin instead of creamy beeswax taper but it'll have to do. Lights it from one of the others, letting her hand make the choice. The candles shiver in unison.

She passes the slip of paper and pencil to her child to scribble the dedication, then posts this blank in the box. She drops a pound coin into the coin box, shattering the silence.

A last look back at the candle (flame pulling upwards, must be a hole in the roof) and they leave the man to his prayer or his thoughts, eyes closed again now, and return to the outside doors, even her soft-soled shoes sounding on the tiles.

Over the crossing – the kerbstones' crystalline glint – and back onto their own road, more and more pumpkins out now and windows dressed, in the time it took them to buy the apples and light a flame. Pre-printed notices up, from the Neighbourhood Watch – no trick-or-treaters please. A little curmudgeonly really – everyone here knows not to knock at an unlanterned door.

Japanese anemone in one of the front gardens, gone to seed – dried and skeletal, with a pockmarked head. She reaches an arm in and snaps some off for the window. Juicy fat spiders wait in the middle of webs three feet wide, tensile and glistening, the ends caught on hedges, railings, telegraph poles. Big enough to snag a human.

The sun really setting now, a red glow at the vanishing point. Little legs getting tired, so she carries her child (getting heavier all the time) the last fifty yards, apple bags hanging from her elbows and bumping her knees as she walks, and she feels the fine mist hanging in the air like a veil.

She sets down the child and the bags in the porchway, turns the key in the stiff lock, shoves the warped wood, and they go in.

First, they warm some milk on the hob and fire up the grill – the oven door left open to heat the room – and have a cup of tepid milk and a cup of weak tea and a plate of toast in the half-light of the kitchen. She hadn't noticed how icy her hands had got, even the held one, the bones chilled.

They wash and polish the apples and pile them into a stockpot. She snips nets of chocolate coins and tips these in as well, arranging them to gleam metallic amongst the fruit.

They carry the stockpot through to the front room (dim now, daylight fading), unpack the carrier bag and lay the contents ready on the floor below the window – the lantern, a baby's mitten, the horse chestnut leaf, the new conker, a dry rattle of ash keys, the leaves of the maple (blood red), a beech leaf like a blood-red heart, twigs of Japanese anemone, rowanberries – and pour from a Kilner jar all the conkers they've found since late August – some shrivelled and rocklike, soaked in vinegar and baked in the oven, some shiny, one of them still in its spiny case. And a little wooden toy figurine she bought when she was pregnant – a jolly farmer in scarecrow dress, broad-brimmed cloth hat and patched brown jacket.

They dress themselves – grey tights and a grey rollneck for her child, a grey balaclava with ears and a grey tail. Whiskers and a black nose painted on. For herself, a dress from the back of the wardrobe, crushed velvet, cool to the touch, shiny and liquid, the colour of blackberry juice, and a sugar paper hat. Quick look in the bathroom mirror, cabinet flashing as she shuts it.

She opens the front door (its shadow arcs across the threshold) and turns the porch light on, outside air brushing her arms, a tremor of hairs, a hint of tobacco on the breeze. She turns it up to its brightest yellow.

Back in the dim room the chimney breast casts a pall. She flicks the light on and starts to dress the window.

Places joss cones – cypress and cedarwood – in a small china dish. Fetches matches, strikes one and dips the flame so it touches them; they catch and burn out and glow, filling the window with indigo smoke as well as light.

The cauldron with its fruit and coins left ready in the hallway. The pumpkin, with its manic goblin visage, centred on the sill. Checks the display from outside. Steps backward and glances down the road: the vista hazy, vaporous, indistinct. Bites into an apple. Holds it in her teeth while she adjusts the bats, rechecks. Snaps off the overhead light in the room and sees the forms of moths on the glass, inside and outside, drawn to the beacon.

Her child creeps closer now and she can feel the warmth drift onto her, arms round her neck. Perfume and grit of the incense. She leans back into the arms and her eyelids flutter closed for a moment, willing sleep.

A smoky grey cat jumps onto the sill, eyes glowing at the window, the knock of its nose on the glass and the whiskers bending. Eyes them suspiciously a while, then jumps down into the dark behind the bins.

There's something else outside: a toddler peering round the hedge. Two years old, the shape looks familiar. Dressed in green, brown face paint on its cheeks, satin hood drawn snugly round the face, and a cloak with spines – she's not sure what it's meant to be, perhaps a hedgehog, or a monster. She beckons it – it comes closer. The shape is definitely familiar – those slight shoulders, sloping a little, almost unformed. It's drawn to the window, to the lantern – *to the toy farmer*. It presses against the glass and traces a finger around the toy through the pane. She gets up gently and picks up the figure; the child draws back from the window – she must look like a giant. She quickly steps out of the room, to the hall, to the door and opens it just as the child has backed out of the front garden, is nearly back on the pavement. She holds the figure out in her outstretched arm, at the child's height, apple still in her other hand. Tilts it from side to side – a little jig. The child looks at it. Takes a small step forward. She tilts it again, takes another bite from her apple. The child looks up at her. It's wearing a brown rollneck and its cape is lined with white. Oh, she says. You're a conker! She laughs. I've been waiting for you, she says, and she holds the door open.

146

WHAT'S FOR YOU
WON'T GO BY YOU

Ollie watches Ria measure out the dose. Give us a swig, he says.

He sees a calculation running behind the screen of her eyes. A tightening at the corners of the mouth. She stretches across the space between them, hands him the little paper cup, slowly.

He looks at her over the top of it, pauses a moment, takes a tiny green sip.

Ria shakes her head at him. Lightweight.

He smiles, returns it and she finishes it.

She settles back in her armchair, feet tucked under her, and chucks him a tobacco tin. Roll us one, love.

He squeezes the lid, pulls out the stuff – she's got an old mechanical roller in there, and some hash.

She watches him roll. Come down the needle exchange with me tomorrow?

Am I staying then?

It's a long way home, isn't it?

He licks the paper. What do you need needles for?

I don't but, you know, they're free. She stretches across to take the cig from him. Condoms too. Might need those. She picks a candle off the occasional table for a light, blows out smoke. They give you a cup of tea there.

With four sugars. And a plastic spoon. He takes a new paper and rolls one for himself.

He looks around him. The aesthetic goes with the architecture: tidy, vacuumed and polished, matching furniture in orange-coloured wood, plump cushions in pretty colours, shagpile rugs. A cut-glass fruit bowl (circa 1970) filled with gerbera heads and floating candles graces the glass-topped table to his left. There's a faint smell that might be air freshener.

Your flat looks nice, he says. Nicer than mine.

Heroin, best career move I ever made.

He finds a lighter in the tin. You signing on?

Don't have to any more. I've got a line.

Oh yeah? What sort of a line?

Ha ha. What do you want to drink?

Whisky.

With an e or without?

Um, without.

She opens a cabinet, gets out tumblers and a bottle, pours and hands him one. What was the private view anyway?

Site-specific at Bold Tendencies.

Oh yeah I know it. Rye Lane car park.

That's the one.

She rolls her eyes. I can remember when SLG was a shithole.

Still is.

So how was it, the show?

All very chi-chi.

Isn't it?

I never knew Peckham had so many white people.

I think they bus them in. She stubs out her cigarette, walks over and takes the tin from him, holds up the hash.

He nods.

She goes back to her chair and lays out papers for a joint. Come to Wimbledon with me?

No.

Centre Court. First Friday.

How come?

Ran into my old boss. Told him I was having chemo. He offered me the pair.

You're not though – are you?

No but, you know, same ballpark. I look like shit anyway. She looks up. Feel free to, you know, deny it.

He narrows his eyes a little and smiles.

You look exactly the same, she says. And then she looks down, turns her attention to the joint.

He flashes up an image of her, sitting in the bath (pink bath), bare light bulb, damp pink bathmat, him – sober, fully clothed, having run over from work when she called – kneeling on the floor, black jeans, black shirt, sleeves rolled up, arms in the bath, the water hot, then cooling, trying to help her find a line. His hands white, knuckles and wrist bone prominent – there was a ring on his finger then, silver. The flesh of his fingertips getting wrinkly after a while. Her flesh magnified by the bathwater, but she always had a surprising amount of flesh packed under her clothes. It surprised him every time. Always quite clean, even when she was using. Although if you have baths every day.

They found one eventually, in her thigh. He pushed the needle in. And then holding her up, supporting her head to make sure she didn't drown, his shirt getting soaked – no point rolling those sleeves. Damp patches on the knees of his jeans. He pulled the plug. Watched the water drain away while she sat there shivering.

He shakes his head, looks around him for a cigarette. She has the tin. His are in his jacket.

She sparks the joint and leans back in her chair. A clairvoyant told me I'd see you again one day. He was a witch doctor actually.

He looks at his hands, his wrists: his own veins, clear and blue, then up at her.

Wanna take this? She holds out the joint.

He stretches over, takes it with the tips of his fingers.

She pours another whisky. He holds out his glass and she tops it up.

You look good, he says. Your flat looks good. You look good. He hands back the joint. So what are you doing, he says. These days.

Hospital. Pharmacy. Shop. Pub.

He drinks his whisky. They pass the joint back and forth in silence.

Did you go back to Goldsmiths, he says, although he knows the answer.

She gives him a steady look. No.

She holds up the last bit of roach.

He shakes his head. Chuck us the tin, he says, and he rolls two more cigarettes.

So what about you, she says.

You know. Art reviews, private views. The occasional lemonade. Nothing very exciting.

She shakes her head at him. Gonna do something with that degree of yours then?

Gonna get that degree of yours then?

Oh, you know me, Ollie. Take it a day at a time. The sun is shining. I'm drug free. What's your excuse?

He lifts his hand up, spreads the fingers.

You let me introduce you to my parents, you fuck. You let me introduce you to my son.

It was a long fucking time ago, Ria.

A pause.

How is he? Tom.

Fuck off.

He lays his head back in the chair.

I could have done it then, she says. When we were twenty-five. Not so much now.

It hasn't been much fun for me either.

So you fucked up your own life too, is that what you're trying to say? Well. I played no part in that.

Never said you did.

You know he asked about you. Is Ollie coming with you again, Mam? Oh don't worry, he doesn't any more. He's sixteen now. He doesn't even ask about me.

Shit, is he really sixteen?

She grabs a pillar candle – interesting choice of missile – and throws it at his head. He ducks and it smashes to pieces on the wall behind him.

After a safe interval he turns to look at the bits of wax on the floor, still keeping one eye on Ria. You still could, you know, he says. Finish your degree.

Yeah yeah. Mature students. I know.

She stares into space a moment and then stands and leaves the room.

He hears bath water running. She comes back in. I'm gonna have a bath. Do you want to get in with me?

He shuts his eyes, opens them again, and runs his fingers round his eye sockets.

Scared of getting hep C?

Probably already got it.

Your liver's fucked either way.

Yeah.

What then?

He breathes in. Out. Dunno.

I'm gonna light some candles. She takes a stack of tealights from the top of the television.

He follows her into the bathroom and sits on the edge of the bathtub. The bath still pink (course it is). Do you want a line?

She takes the mirror off the wall. Toothpaste-spattered. I forgot how out of it you need to be.

No, I just feel like a line.

How often do you do it?

I dunno. But I've got 10p in my bank account. So not that often.

Still working at the old place? She tips a bottle of essential oil into the water.

Yeah.

Same job?

Yep. He unbuttons his cuffs.

They ever give you that pay rise?

Nope.

He takes his shirt off. She stops talking.

He has a sudden urge to vomit. He blinks it away, breathes in, breathes out. He takes out the bag and looks around him for a blade.

On the windowsill, she says. What was that for then – the private view?

You never know, do you.

Got my own straws, she says, and takes two out of a box.

He cuts two thin lines, does one. Ria does the other. She stands for a moment dabbing her nose. The water is boiling now, the bathroom steaming up.

She takes another bottle of oil and drips it in. This is for calming thoughts, she says: lavender. Frankincense: apotropaic. And this is rosemary: comfort for the living, peace for the dead.

She undresses and climbs into the bath.

★

The room is sunny, curtains and windows open. Ria isn't there. He wanders through to the living room and opens the balcony door. He goes into the kitchen. There's something stinking in a jar lying sideways on a tray – some kind of mouldy plant-experiment – but it looks purposeful, so he leaves it. Maybe she's starting a cannabis farm. He puts the kettle on and goes through the cupboards. Green fucking tea leaves in a tin. Chamomile and honey. What look like dried jasmine flowers in another. After a search he finds some normal tea. In the fridge: Interferon. Ribavirin. A takeaway carton of chow mein, almost full. He sniffs it and prods it, peering at the edges for signs of mould, then begins to eat.

The front door goes and Ria comes in, arms laden with plain white carrier bags.

Oh Christ, don't eat that, that's been in there a week.

She grabs it out of his hand and chucks it in the bin. She piles her groceries onto the worktop – paper bags warm with breadstuffs, avocados, bananas, milk, coffee, cigarettes, biscuits, *The Mirror*.

Ollie warms his hands on a bakery bag, then pulls off a piece of the loaf and chews it.

I'll make us coffee, she says, and takes down an espresso pot.

153

What the fuck is that, Ria? He gestures to the plant-experiment.

Oh, that. I'm sprouting my own mung beans, it's addictive. They're really good for you.

She fills the pot and lights the gas.

In the kitchen's bright daylight fine lines are visible around her eyes, and the odd grey hair. Her skin looks a little thicker than it used to.

Hard paper round, she says.

She hands him a bag of pastries and he follows her through to the balcony. She throws a rug down on the floor, laying it with cups and sugar, and spreads out cushions. It's sunny with a cool breeze, and the balcony faces south. A couple of geraniums in tubs are beginning to flower. She takes the full ashtray away and brings back a clean one, with the pot of coffee.

She pours for them both, and unwraps a new pack of Embassy, offering him one and lighting them with a Bic.

He sips the coffee and draws in smoke. Hot coffee, strong fags, bright sun, cool air. He lies back on a cushion.

You roll, I'll deal. She nudges the tobacco tin over to him.

Oh not just yet. Let me have a fag first.

Ria picks up the newspaper and leafs through it.

What's going on in the world, then?

Same old shit. Do you want your horoscope?

No, I'd rather not know. He stubs out his cigarette and takes an almond pastry.

You gonna roll or will I?

You if you want one. Is there more coffee?

Tiny bit in the pot. OK, gonna deal my cards first. She goes into the living room and returns with a pack of angel cards.

She shuffles, an inward look on her face. She shuts her eyes. After a minute she puts a card down on the rug, with a decisive flick. She shuffles some more, and then deals another, then a third. She opens her eyes and sets down the pack, looking over the cards she has dealt.

What do they say? he says.

Hang on. She shakes a cigarette out of the packet and lights it, blowing smoke out in a long stream as she reads the cards. OK.

What?

She gathers them up and jiggles them back into the pack, shuffling once. Come down the health food shop with me later?

What for?

St John's Wort. You should try it you know.

Fucking hell.

It works.

★

The health food shop is large, and bright with strip lights. Surprising that the local population could support it.

The cashier recognizes Ria, and they exchange hellos. Ollie and Ria make their way along the aisles.

Have they got any snake oil, d'you think?

Shh. Here we are. St John's Wort. She picks up a bulk pack.

As they pass the essential oils she palms a couple of tiny bottles and slips them into her pocket.

Ollie makes a panorama of the store, taking in but avoiding looking at the fish-eye mirrors and swivelling cameras. Hey look, red quinoa, he says, picking up a cellophane package and showing her, then elaborately replacing it on the shelf.

It's a bit expensive, she says. Although it is meant to be good for you. She picks it up and reads the label. Lots of vitamins. I don't want to carry too much now though. Think I'll stick with the St John's Wort.

155

Oh and I'll have this please, she says, picking up a *Psychologies* magazine by the till.

She pays for the goods in her hands and they go out and cross the road.

There's our bus, says Ria, and they run and jump on.

★

They are buzzed in before they have a chance to press the buzzer. The door closes behind them and they climb the stairs.

A pretty, dark-haired girl behind the needle-hatch serves them: she seems to know Ria. Half Italian or Turkish maybe. She clocks Ollie – large, lined eyes – gives him an in-your-dreams-mate look. Yes, well. The canteen-lounge, with its doss-house vibe, looks just the same: huge, battered sofas and bright kitchen, tea urn on the counter, its fuse boosted with aluminium foil (they like to live dangerously here). There is a quantity of smashed crockery in the open bin and fragments in the dustpan. It's quiet – too early for most. Someone – a member of the back-room staff, in smart trousers, shirt and sweater, smart glasses – is having a fag on the fire escape at the far end, letting the cool air in. She glances over as she sees them come into the big room, finishes quickly, shuts the fire door and walks back through to the office. A nice man behind the canteen counter makes them a cup of tea – ah yes, the plastic spoons.

No sugar please, says Ollie quickly, and the man looks up, surprised. Like he wants to look Ollie up and down, but stops himself.

Two for me please, says Ria.

The man puts on latex gloves and mops down the counters with disinfectant, and gives their coffee table a wipe with the same solution. It leaves a hospital smell. The table is scarred with old cigarette burns.

Would you like some biscuits, he says, and brings them over,

156

four Rich Tea on an institutional dish. You're doing well Ria, he says as he sets them down.

Thanks, she says. Nearly a year now. Ria puts the paper bag of condoms down on the table and dunks a biscuit in her tea. He used to listen to me every week, she says, when the man has gone. She sinks back into the sofa with her biscuits, kicks off her shoes and rests her feet on Ollie's legs, digging in her toes.

He shifts round to face her and puts his feet up too. The sofa is amazingly comfortable: it would be quite nice to sleep here until closing time, whenever that is.

★

Let's get lunch, says Ria. I'll get it.

It must be mid afternoon. They stop at a Chinese takeaway and she orders chow mein and prawn crackers, two pairs of chopsticks and two cans of Fanta. They eat it on the grass in Kennington Park. Ria reads her magazine (the front cover: Have You Given Away Your Power? Claim it Back).

A street drinker approaches and she gives him her change. That's all I've got, I'm afraid. Here, have these. She gives him the remainder of the prawn crackers.

She wipes the chopsticks on the paper napkin and sticks them in her hair, bundling it up. She takes out her tobacco tin and rolls a joint.

★

The band is good – at least, they seem to know what they're doing, so far as Ollie can tell.

It's years since he's been down here – not since the cigarette ban. He remembers the old priest smoking fag after fag – sitting in the corner, lank grey hair falling to his dog collar, tapping his feet, black Derby shoes and fine dress socks, that thin smile he had that was almost a leer, peddling jazz and hallucinogens. (How did they banish the smell of smoke in time for the mornings? Must have been people praying here, kneeling on squashed chips and fag butts and beer-drenched hassocks. How d'you explain that, Father Rodney? To your other congregation? The Body of Christ. The Blood of Christ. And that's a squashed chip.)

Do they still sell absinthe here?

Not for years.

The electric candles are atmospheric. The darkness feels smoky, even without the smoke. He can make out words carved in the stone slabs under his feet: they must be tombs.

The barman seems to know Ria. She gets them beers.

The double bassist really is good (at least: he looks and sounds convincing, and there are people in hats and black turtlenecks nodding approvingly and occasionally vocalizing). A younger priest mingles with the aficionados, the black garb blending in nicely. No sign of the old guy.

Around them people are eating burgers and plates of pasta at candlelit tables, seated at pews.

Ria looks enviously at the food. Shall we get dinner here?

I've only got a twenty. I was thinking booze.

We could get chips on the way home.

I'll get another round. Shall we have shots?

There's a bit you can dance to (sort of) and they try to dance to it. A golden, airy sound and a definite beat though it skips about and you miss it.

★

Back on the number 36 again. Or is it the number 12. One of them will get them there, one of them won't and they'll have to remember to get off. Leave it to Ria. She's the one who lives here. She knows where she lives.

★

She throws the chips at him, the whole bag hitting him hot in the face and falling to the ground, scattered over the pavement – like wood shavings, like petals. He would have eaten those.

Ria screams and screams.

A stocky man passing by slows and looks at them and Ollie puts his hands up – It's alright, he says. It's alright.

★

Ollie sits on the floor. She comes back into the room in her dressing gown. She pours out her methadone, concentrating hard not to spill it, and knocks it back. She breaks a vitamin capsule into a cold-cream pot, scoops out a handful and smears it thickly over her face, a white mask. Like Noh theatre. She rubs Bach Rescue Remedy into her temples, making a circular motion.

The flat is burning with candles, worse than ever: he can feel the heat off them, smell the wax mixed in with the smell of cold cream and essential oils. Ria is singing now, a Kirsty MacColl song – she resembles her a little – performing as if on a stage, fag in hand. She would fare quite well on a TV talent show. He wonders that she's never thought of it. He would phone in and vote for her. She lifts up her hands.

The angel cards are scattered at their feet. The one next to Ollie's toe reads:

HEALING THE PAST

This card comes to you because there's a recurring pattern that stems from hurt feelings in your past. It's time for you to change this pattern by facing and healing old emotional pain. You may feel tired of revisiting the same issues yet believe that there's no other way.

He is tired of it. Really tired. What would happen if he knocked over one of these candles now? Or the methadone: how much would be a good dose? If he drank it, would they replace it for her? They wouldn't leave her high and dry, would they? Surely? It must happen a lot.

Another card lies face down. He hesitates a moment, turns it over:

RELEASE AND SURRENDER

We shower you with blessings of our radiant love. Open your arms, and release the challenges that you've held tightly gripped within your hands. Open your hands, arms and heart to our love and assistance.

BACKGAMMON

Suzy opens her massive wallet and pulls out a paint sample. She ting-ting-tings her glass with a nail. 'Now, your attention please. I'm trying to decide between these shades. For an east-facing living room.' She lays it on the picnic table in front of me.

I haul myself up to a sitting position, legs still stretched along the bench, and drag the Foster's ashtray over to me. I pick up the card and focus on the small coloured oblongs.

'And then one of these' – another paint sample – 'for the woodwork. Late Victorian.'

Dave says, 'Lara should come to dinner.'

'Oh yes – we need a guest to motivate us.'

'And we'd love to have you. How about next Saturday. Are you free?'

'Unusually and unexpectedly, I am.' I say this through a smile. Suzy winks at me and reaches over to help herself to one of my cigarettes, scrunching up her own packet.

'Eight o'clock, then,' says Dave, finishing his pint. Ours are still full.

'I look forward to it.'

'Dave will cook. I can't.' She pats his chest. She digs out another sample card. 'Or we could go rogue with the woodwork and choose one of these.'

She eyes me expectantly.

I dutifully study the shortlisted candidates ringed in biro.

'Well, anyway, you'll see it. Although it looks different in the evening. But it has to work in various lights, of course.'

She takes the samples back, files them away behind the banknotes. 'Oh, and I like this' – an inch of cloth stapled to a card – 'for the curtains. It has to be curtains because of the style of the property.'

Through the open doorway Dave signals to the barman and raises his empty glass. A new one is brought and he pays and drinks it in three long draughts.

I play with a beer mat. Then I notice it's been chewed, so I leave it.

Dave slaps his hands on the table. 'I'm going to Tesco. Anything else we need?'

'I sent you the list this morning.'

'I know you did, that's why I'm asking: anything else since then? Do we need eggs?'

Suzy smiles and shakes her head. 'See you at home, darling.' She raises her face for his kiss.

'Right. Well.' He nods. He looks at me and there's something at the back of his eyes. (What is it – shame? Guilt?)

I tip my glass at him and say, in dismissal, 'Enjoy Tesco.'

He looks back at me. (Jealousy, even?) There's a pause, and then he goes, freeing us up to talk about his sperm – motility of, as affected by diet and underwear. I throw my legs back onto the bench and wedge my bag under my feet for extra elevation, but Suzy's oblivious. She's four years older than I am, so I can see what's ahead. She has a band of fine lines across her nose and cheekbones.

As it starts to get cooler we move inside and settle at a table in the corner. Suzy asks after my leg but she's got a faraway look and I can tell her heart's not in it.

'We had a row a couple of weeks ago,' she says. 'I left him and stayed in a hotel for the night. That's the first time I've done that.'

I take a deep breath. 'What was the row about?'

★

At eleven, I see Dave appear in the doorway to fetch Suzy back from the pub.

'Talk of the devil,' I say.

'Time to come home,' he says.

Suzy's merry again by now. 'Lara hasn't finished her drink,' she says.

'Well, Lara can sit here and finish if she wants to, but we're going home.'

'Darling, aren't we going to walk her to the bus stop?'

'If she comes now. Otherwise I'm sure she can make her own way.'

'It's alright, I've finished,' I say, downing the rest.

'Do you need us to walk you to the bus stop, Lara?' says Dave.

'No, I'm fine on my own.'

'Don't forget dinner next Saturday,' he says, baring his teeth in a smile.

★

I arrive at five past eight. Suzy opens the door with a cheer and wafts me in. I hand over a bottle and some chocolates and we go into the lounge. She's watching a TV talent show.

163

Dave pokes his head and shoulders through the serving hatch. He looks too tall and bulky for the galley kitchen. He's wearing a butcher's apron and a back-to-front baseball cap.

'Hello Lara,' he smiles ingratiatingly, waving a spatula. 'Welcome.'

'Dave's a brilliant cook,' says Suzy. 'He learned to cook in the army.'

'We're having stuffed peppers and lamb,' says Dave, 'followed by pears poached in wine.'

'Perfect,' I say.

'Pour Lara a glass,' says Suzy.

'Thanks,' I say. 'I'll have the white.'

Dave passes it through the hatch.

'I love this show,' says Suzy, laughing. 'I vote for someone every week.'

'Do you watch it, Lara?' says Dave.

'I'm not usually in on a Saturday night,' I say, and then, in case that sounds too smug: 'You know, single girl.'

'Why don't you give Lara the tour?' says Dave.

'Would you like the tour?' says Suzy.

'Yes, I would.'

She leads me up the hallway. 'The kitchen's too small really, but it does for now.'

Dave goes into the lounge and switches off the television.

'I like what you've done with the flooring,' I say.

'Oh you noticed.' She smiles. 'Yes, I'm pleased with it. This is our room.' She opens the door. 'And here's the spare room. You can stay tonight if you like, if it gets late. I put fresh bedding on the other day.'

'Thanks. I'll see how drunk I get.'

'Here's the bathroom. And here's the utility room. It really makes up for the size of the kitchen. We even have a little garden through here.' She unlocks the back door.

Outside it's peaceful, a picture of domesticity complete with washing line and bird table. 'It's sweet,' I say, stepping down onto the lawn. My heels sink into the earth. 'Is that a pear tree?'

'I think so, but it's young. I don't know if we'll be here long enough for it to fruit.'

It's a lovely evening. I suggest that we sit outside for a while, and offer to fetch the wine. In the kitchen, Dave's spooning rice mixture into peppers. 'We're in the garden,' I say, taking the bottle out of the fridge, and carry it back through the flat to Suzy. We sit on the lawn and smoke. I take off my shoes and the grass prickles the arches of my feet.

'I hope you stay here,' I say. 'In town at least.'

'We want to buy a house. I'd really like to get somewhere and start doing it up, but for the time being…' She sighs. 'A flat in town makes more sense.'

Dave appears in the doorway.

'Talk of the devil,' I say.

'Dinner is served,' he says.

We go back through to the lounge. He's set up a dining table next to the serving hatch. It's laid with bamboo mats and large earthenware plates and three covered dishes.

'You didn't put out the goblets?' says Suzy. 'I wanted goblets.'

'I don't know where they are,' says Dave. 'In a box somewhere. Everyone's got a glass anyway.' Dave fumbles in his pocket and lights the candles.

'Sit down,' says Suzy, gesturing my place.

Dave goes to the kitchen and comes back wearing oven gloves and carrying another casserole dish. He removes the covers and serves out peppers, lamb chops, ratatouille and green beans.

'This looks beautiful,' I say.

Dave tops up my wine.

'I shouldn't drink too much,' says Suzy. 'My medication.'

'Doesn't normally stop you,' says Dave.

'To life,' says Suzy, raising her glass.

After dinner Dave clears away the plates and puts on coffee. Suzy breaks out the chocolates.

'Shall we play a game? Let's play a game!' She jumps up and opens a cabinet. 'Dave and I go to that pub where they have board games. You just ask at the bar for a chess set. We play for hours! We played backgammon all night the other week. I got so drunk Dave had to carry me home.'

'Backgammon,' I say. 'I haven't played that in years. Don't know anyone who knows how to play it.'

'We play it! I can't believe you never said. Dave's brilliant at backgammon. Did we never go to the board-game pub with you?'

'You did,' I say. 'We sat outside and got drunk and never asked for a game.'

'We've got a set! Do you want to play?'

'Yes, I'd love to. It really has been years. I warn you, I'm pretty good.'

'Play her, Dave! I tell you, he is brilliant.' She gets out the board and opens it up on the dining table.

'I'll let you play her first,' Dave says.

I play Suzy and win quite easily. Dave smokes as he watches us.

'You are pretty good!' says Suzy. 'This could be a long game. Wait!' She jumps up, grabs a wooden bowl from the kitchen and empties a packet of pistachios into it. She gets down three tumblers, ice cubes and a bottle of raki and pours us each a generous measure. Then she sits down at the table and smiles.

Dave and I sit opposite each other.

I rub my hands together.

Suzy hands me the counters and I set them up on my side.

I crack pistachios as Dave lines up his men. I roll a six. He rolls a two. I begin.

'Have you played for money?' he says, in all seriousness, eyeballing me as he shakes the dice in his cup.

I smile, leaning forward with my chin on my hand. 'No, but I've played old men in Turkey.'

He leaves a blot and I hit it. He rolls and can't move. Suzy gets up and changes the music, asking what we want. 'Something Turkish,' I say. Dave picks up his cup and shakes it next to his ear.

'It's my turn,' I say.

He looks at me. 'Is it?' He puts the cup down and I roll.

Ten minutes later he's in trouble again.

'You have to move,' I say.

'Can't,' he says.

'You can move the three,' I say. It leaves another blot exposed. 'I'll go easy on you.'

He looks at me. And then he moves, slowly.

I pick up the pace. Two rolls later I bear off the first of my men. Roll, move. Roll, move-move. I throw a double five and bear off four more.

Suzy watches, engrossed.

Dave picks up his tumbler and nods his head towards the bottle. 'Pour us another, babe.' He rolls. She turns and pours him a drink. He moves.

'You're cheating,' I say.

'No I'm not.'

I raise an eyebrow. 'You threw a ten and you moved twelve.'

'No I didn't.'

'You were there and there.'

167

'I was there and *there*.' He stabs the board with his index finger. 'Come on.'

'I didn't fucking cheat.'

I laugh openly. He looks like he's about to hit me. Instead he upsets the board. The men fly into the air. There's a silence. Raki drips from the table.

'Oops,' I say.

He gets up, charges into the hallway, picks up his jacket and storms out. The front door shakes on its hinges. I take a sip of my wine. Suzy sits there, not moving.

'You'd better go,' she says eventually.

'Yep.' I get up and fish my phone out of my bag. 'I'll call myself a cab. It's been a lovely evening.'

'I mean now. Before he goes and has a drink. Otherwise he won't come home at all.'

I let that hang in the air.

'I'll ring him and tell him that you've gone.'

'OK.' I find my shoes and slip them on, losing my balance slightly as I stand. I didn't bring flats.

She follows me to the door as I put my jacket on and wind my scarf around my neck. I take my time.

'That's a pretty scarf,' she says. I don't say anything.

'I'm sorry,' she says firmly as she closes the door.

It's a mild night with a fine drizzle. I check the clock – quarter to one – and head towards the main drag, dialling the number for the cab. My leg's starting to bother me again. I take a short cut. Up ahead of me, in the middle of the road, I see Dave, urinating in an arc.

ACKNOWLEDGEMENTS

I am very happy to acknowledge financial awards from the Society of Authors (Authors' Foundation) and from Arts Council England.

I would like to thank my publishers and editors at Galley Beggar, Sam Jordison and Eloise Millar.

I'd also like to thank the editors of the publications in which these stories first appeared: Ellah Wakatama Allfrey, Brendan Barrington, Joe Melia, Euan Monaghan and Kay Brugmans, Susheila Nasta, Joyce Russell, Jacques Testard and Ben Eastham, Susan Tomaselli, and Tom Vowler.

Thanks also to Matthew Krishanu, Aisha Phoenix and Julian Poidevin for being the manuscript's astute first readers; to Cathy Galvin and The Word Factory, Eva Lewin and Spread the Word, and Amy Zamarripa Solis and Writing Our Legacy, for their longstanding support; to Alison MacLeod and Nicholas Royle for valuable feedback and advice; to Talha Ahsan; and to the archivist and librarians of the Vestry House Museum.

GALLEY BEGGAR PRESS

We hope that you've enjoyed *English Magic*. If you would like to find out more about Uschi, along with some of her fellow authors, head to www.galleybeggar.co.uk.

There, you will also find information about our subscription scheme, 'Galley Buddies', which is there to ensure we can continue to put out ambitious and unusual books like *English Magic*.

Subscribers to Galley Beggar Press:

· Receive limited black cover editions of our future titles (printed in a one-time run of 500).

· Have their names included in a special acknowledgement section at the back of our books.

· Are sent regular updates and invitations to our book launches, talks and other events.

· Enjoy a 20% discount code for the purchase of any of our backlist (as well as for general use throughout our online shop).

WHY BE A GALLEY BUDDY?

At Galley Beggar Press we don't want to compromise on the excellence of the writing we put out, or the physical quality of our books. We've also enjoyed numerous successes and prize nominations since we set up, in 2012. Almost all of our authors have gone on to be longlisted, shortlisted, or the winners of over twenty of the world's most prestigious literary awards.

But publishing for the sake of art is a risky commercial strategy. In order to keep putting out the very best books we can, and to continue to support talented writers, we need your help. The money we receive from our Galley Buddy scheme is an essential part of keeping us going.

By becoming a Galley Buddy, you help us to launch and foster a new generation of writers.

To join today, head to:
https://www.galleybeggar.co.uk/subscribe

Galley Beggar Press would like to thank the following individuals, without the generous support of whom our books would not be possible:

Ann Abineri
Kémy Ade
Timothy Ahern
Andrew Ainscough
Sam Ainsworth
Jez Aitchison
Simon Andrup
Callum Akaas
Ayodeji Alaka
Joseph H Alexander
Carol Allen
Richard Allen
Lulu Allison
Barbaros Altug
Kirk Annett
Eleanor Anstruther
Ebba Aquila
Elizabeth Aquino
Deborah Arata
Darryl Ardle
Robert Armiger
Sheila Armstrong
Sean Arnold
Curt Arnson
Xanthe Ashburner
Bethany Ashley
Robert Ashton
Adrian Astur
    Alvarez
Edmund Atrill
Vaida Aviks
Jo Ayoubi
Kerim Aytac
Claire Back
Andrew Bailey
Dexter Bailey
Tom Bailey
Edward Baines
Dawn Baird
Stephen Baird
Glynis Baker
Andrea Barlien
Chad Barnes
Ian Bartlett

Phil Bartlett
Rachel Beale
James Beavis
Rachel Bedder
Joseph Bell
Angel Belsey
Felicity Bentham
Michelle Best
Gary Betts
David Bevan
Alison Bianchi
Benjamin Bird
Sandra Birnie
Peter Blackett
Matt Blackstock
Adam Blackwell
Melissa Blaschke
Lynne Blundell
David Boddy
Sophie Boden
John Bogg
Heleen Boons
Nicholas Bouskill
Poppy Boutell
Edwina Bowen
Michelle Bowles
Joanna Bowman
David Bradley
Sean Bradley
Andrew J. Bremner
Aisling Brennan
Joan Brennan
Amanda Bringans
Erin Britton
Julia Brocking
Ben Brooks
Dean Brooks
Lily Brown
Sheila Browse
Peter Brown
Carrie Brunt
Richard Bryant
Justine Budenz
Lesley Budge

Laura Bui
Tony Burke
Kevin Burrell
Alister Burton
Bryan Burton
Joyce Butler
Barbara Byar
Barry Byrne
Rebecca Café
Max Cairnduff
Alan Calder
June Caldwell
Lloyd Calegan
Christopher Caless
Alfric Campbell
Mark Campbell
Laura Canning
Joanna Cannon
Annette Capel
Rhian Capener
Thomas Carlisle
Leona Carpenter
Sean Carroll
Richard Carter
Shaun Carter
Stuart Carter
Soraya Cary
Liam Casey
Leigh Chambers
David Charles
Richard Chatterton
Marcus Cheetham
Rose Chernick
Lina Christopoulou
Neal Chuang
Neil Churchill
Enrico Cioni
Douglas
    Clarke-Williams
Steve Clough
Paul Cole
Faith Coles
Jennifer Coles
John Coles

Emma Coley
Sam Coley
Tonia Collett
Gordon Collins
Gerard Connors
Helene Conrady
Joe Cooney
Kenneth Cooper
Sarah Corbett
Paul Corry
Andy Corsham
Mary Costello
Sally Cott
Nick Coupe
Andrew Cowan
Diarmuid Cowan
Felicity Cowie
Isabelle Coy-Dibley
Matthew Craig
Nick Craske
Anne Craven
Emma Crawford
Anne-Marie
    Creamer
Alan Crilly
Joanna Crispin
Ian Critchley
Brenda Croskery
James Cross
Kate Crowcroft
Miles Crowley
Stephen Cuckney
Damian Cummings
Stephen Cummins
Andrew Cupples
HC
Emma Curtis Lake
Chris Cusack
Siddharth Dalal
Elisa Damiani
Rachel Darling
Rupert Dastur
Claudia Daventry
Mark Davidson

Harriet Davies
Jessica Davies
Julie Davies
Linda Davies
Nickey Davies
Paul Davies
Alice Davis
Joshua Davis
Toby Day
Robin Deitch
Rebecca Demaree
Stanislaus Dempsey
Paul Dettmann
Turner Docherty
William Dobson
Dennis Donathan
Kirsty Doole
Kelly Doonan
Oliver Dorostkar
David Douce
Janet Dowling
Kelly Downey
Jamie Downs
Guy Dryburgh-Smith
Ian Dudley
Fiona Duffy
Florian Duijsens
Anthony Duncan
Antony Dunford
Stanka Easton
David Edwards
Nicola Edwards
Lance Ehrman
Jonathan Elkon
Ben Ellison
Ian Ellison
Thomas Ellmer
Stefan Erhardt
Alice Erskine
Fiona Erskine
Simeon Esper
Paul Ewen
Adam Fales
Monique Fare
Sarah Farley
Lori Feathers
Gerard Feehily
Jeremy Felt
Timothy Fenech
Vitcoria Fendall
Michael Fenton

Charles Fernyhough
Edward J. Field
Paul Fielder
Joy Finlayson
Elizabeth Finn
Catriona Firth
Becky Fisher
Fitzcarraldo Editions
Holly Fitzgerald
Eleanor Fitzsimons
Alexander Fleming
Grace Fletcher-Hackwood
Hayley Flockhart
Nicholas Flower
Patrick Foley
James Fourniere
Ceriel Fousert
Richard Fradgley
Pauline France
Matthew Francis
Frank Francisconi
Emily Fraser
Annette Freeman
Emma French
Ruth Frendo
Melissa Fu
Graham Fulcher
Paul Fulcher
Lew Furber
Stephen Furlong
Michael Furness
Brid Gallagher
Timothy Gallimore
Marc Galvin
Annabel Gaskell
Honor Gavin
Michael Geisser
Phil Gibby
Alison Gibson
Nolan Geoghegan
Neil George
Andy Godber
James Goddard
Stephanie Golding
Elizabeth Goldman Morgan
Golf-French
Matthew Goodman
Sakura Gooneratne

Sara Gore
Nikheel Gorolay
Cathy Goudie
Simon Goudie
Emily Grabham
Paul Greaves
Louise Greenberg
Chris Gribble
Judith Griffith
Neil Griffiths
Ben Griffiths
Vicki Grimshaw
Sam Guglani
Robbie Guillory
Dave Gunning
David Gunning
Andrew Gummerson
Rhys Gwyther
Ian Hagues
Daniel Hahn
Alice Halliday
Peter Halliwell
Karen Hamilton
Emma Hammond
Paul Handley
Rachel Handley
Kirsteen Hardie
Hal Harding-Jones
Vanessa Harris
Jill Harrison
Alice Harvey
Becky Harvey
Shelley Hastings
Simon Hawkesworth
Sarah Hawthorn
Patricia Hayes
David Hebblethwaite
Richard Hemmings
Padraig J. Heneghan
Stu Hennigan
Penelope Hewett Brown
Felix Hewison-Carter
Martin Hickman
Alexander Highfield
Jennifer Hill

Molly Hill
Susan Hill
Daniel Hillman
Rod Hines
Ned Hirst
Alex Hitch
Marcus Hobson
Peter Hodgkinson
Camilla Hoel
Aisling Holling
Tim Hopkins
Shane Horgan
Rashad Hosein
William Hsieh
Hugh Hudson
Anna Jean Hughes
Emily Hughes
Gavin Hughes
Richard Hughes
Robert Hughes
Andy Hunt
Kim-ling Humphrey
Louise Hussey
LJ Hutchins
Simone Hutchinson
Simon Issatt
Joseph Jackson
Paul Jackson
Jane Jakeman
Hayley James
Gareth Jelley
Kavita A. Jindal
Alice Jolly
George Johnson
Jane Johnson
Bevan Jones
Emma Jones
Jupiter Jones
Kerry-Louise Jones
Rebecca Jones
Amy Jordison
Anna Jordison
Diana Jordison
Atul Joshi
Claire Jost
Benjamin Judge
Gary Kaill
Darren Kane
Laura Kaye
Thomas Kealy
Andrew Kelly

Michael Ketchum
Peter Kettle
Jeffrey Kichen
Vijay Khurana
Jacqueline Knott
Amy Koheealiee
Teddy Kristiansen
Elisabeth Kumar
Gage LaFleur
Philip Lane
Domonique Lane-
   Osherov
I Lang
Kathy Lanzarotti
Jackie Law
Jo Lawrence
Sue Lawson
Rick Le Coyte
Carley Lee
Liz and Pete Lee
Darren Lerigo
Joyce Lillie
   Robinson
Yin Lim
Rebecca Lake
Rachel Lalchan
Eric Langley
Catherine Latsis
Elizabeth Leach
Ferdia Lennon
Joanne Leonard
Chiara Levorato
Mark Lewis
Elizabeth Leyland
Christian
   Livermore
Jesse Loncraine
Katie Long
Nick Lord
   Lancaster
Isaac Lowe
Lele Lucas
Sean Lusk
Simona Lyons
Marc Lyth
Jean Mackay
Wendy and Dave
   MacKay
Victoria MacKenzie
Tom MacLean
Andrea Macleod
Duncan Mackie

Brendan Madden
Joseph Maffey
Anne Maguire
Eleanor Maier
Johnny Mains
Philip Makatrewicz
Anil Malhotra
Tom Mandall
Joshua Mandel
Matthew Mansell
Emily Marchant
Chiara Margiotta
John Marr
Natalie Marshall
Paul Marshall
Iain Martin
Amanda Mason
Rosalind May
Philip Maynard
Stephen Maynard
Sally Mayor
Sara McCallum
Amy McCauley
Paul McCombs
Ella McCrystle
Fabia McDougall
Kieran McGrath
Sheila McIntosh
Alan McIntyre
Gerald McWilliams
Victor
   Meadowcraft
Jason Merrells
Andy Merrills
Tina Meyer
Ali Millar
Jacob Millard
Michael Millington
Phillipa Mills
Sally Minogue
Fiona Mitchell
Lotte Mitchell
   Reford
Ian Mond
Fiona Mongredien
Sue Mongredien
Alexander Monker
Alex Moore
Clare Moore
Gary Moore
Michelle
   Moorhouse

Rachael de Moravia
Nigel J. Morgan
Carlos Eduardo
   Morreo
Jackie Morris
Julie Morris
Patrick Morris
Clive Morrison
Donald Morrison
Roger Morrison
David Musgrave
Electra Nanou
Polly Nash
Zosha Nash
Linda Nathan
Tim Neighbour
Amanda Nicholls
Catherine
   Nicholson
Sophia Nixon
Mariah de Nor
Calum
   Novak-Mitchell
Anna Nsubuga
Georgina
   Nugent-Folan
Arif Nurmohamed
James O'Brien
Liam and Wendy
   O'Connor
Rodney O'Connor
Richard Offer
Seb Ohsan-
   Berthelsen
Janet Oliver
Alec Olsen
Laura Oosterbeek
Sheila O'Reilly
Valerie O'Riordan
Liz O'Sullivan
Jack Oxford
Jenny Owen
Steven Palter
Dave Parry
Gary Partington
Debra Patek
Nicholas Paton
   Philip
Ian Patterson
Nigel Paulson
Stephen Pearsall
Alexa Pearson

Rebecca Peer
Jonathan Perks
Connor Perrie
Tom Perrin
Tony Pettigrew
Dan Phillips
Jennifer Pink
Robert Pisani
Ben Plouviez
Louise Pointer
Erin Polmear
James Pomar
Jonathan Pool
Giacomo Pope
Christopher Potter
Ailsa Power
Trine Prescott
Lesley Preston
David Primost
David Prince
Victoria Proctor
Jill Propst
Samuel Pryce
James Puddephatt
Joyce Pugh
Alan Pulverness
Sarah Pybus
Richard Pye
Alex Pykett
Lisa Quattromini
Leng Leng Quek
Shiva Rahbaran
Sim Ralph
Polly Randall
Jane Rawson
Euan Reed
Dawn Rees
Padraig Reidy
Emma Reitano
Barbara Renel
Vasco Resende
Amy Reynolds
Gaynor Reynolds
Annie Rhodes
Alison Riley
Thea Marie
   Rishovd
Laura Roach
Chris Roberts
Stephen Roberts
Rocky and Kat
Liz Roe

Brian Ronan
Angela Rose
Kalina Rose
Wendy Ross
Nathan Rowley
Martin Rowsell
Beverly Rudy
Giles Ruffer
Libby Ruffle
Tomilyn Rupert
Tim Russ
Rebeka Russell
Naben Ruthnum
John Rutter
Tobias Ryan
Amanda Saint
Floriane Sajdak
Alison Sakai
Michael Saler
Himanshu Kamal
   Saliya
Robert Sanderson
Valentina Santolini
Lior Sayada
Liam Scallon
Amy Scarrott
Linde Schaafsma
Robert Scheffel
Jordan Schlipf
Benedict Schofield
Florian Schroiff
Jan Schoones
Ros Schwartz
Nicola Scott
Stephen Robert
   Scott
James Scudamore
Miss Scullion
Darren Seeley
Kelly Selby-Jones
Elie Sharp
Samuel Sharps
Richard Sheehan
Nicola Shepherd
Emma Shore
Larry Sides
Deborah Siddoway
Kate Simpson

Yvonne Singh
Ann Slack
Jay Slayton-Joslin
Ben Smith
Chris Smith
Connor Smith
Hazel Smith
Ian Smith
Kieron Smith
Nicola Smith
Shannon Smith
Tom Smyth
Lisa Solley
Louise Soraya
   Black
Arabella Spencer
Karmen Spiljak
Sarah Spitz
Hannah Spruce
Chiara Spruijt
Connor Stait
Karl Stange
Daniel Staniforth
Cathryn Steele
Gillian Stern
Stewart Stevens
Mark Stevenson
Tabatha Stirling
Dagmara Stoic
Justina Stonyte
Anne Storr
Colette Storrow
Elizabeth Stott
Jochen Stremmel
Julia Stringwell
Andrew Stuart
Zara Stubbs
Daryl Sullivan
Jesse Surridge
Drashti Sutariya
Juliet Sutcliffe
Helen Swain
Helen Symington
Ewan Tant
Sarah Tapp
Justine Taylor
Peter Talor
Moray Teale

Alan Teder
Gill Thackray
Vivienne Thackray
Natalia
   Theodoridou
Cennin Thomas
Sue Thomas
Susannah
   Thompson
Caroline Thomson
Graham Thornelow
Sam Thorp
Nan Tilghman
Matthew Tilt
Amie Tolson
Margaret Tongue
James Torrence
Kate Triggs
Steve Tuffnell
Devin Tupper
Nick Turner
Harriet Tyce
Eleanor Updegraff
Raminta Uselyte
Esther Van Buul
Bart Van Overmeire
Nicole Vanderbilt
David Varley
Francesca
   Veneziano
Irene Verdiesen
Essi Viding
Boris Vidovic
Bea Vincent
Meg Vincent
Gabriel Vogt
Stephen Waderman
Julia Wait
Chris Walker
Phoebe Walker
Stephen Walker
Ben Waller
MJ Wallis
Sinead Walsh
Steve Walsh
David Ward
Jerry Ward
Kate Ward

Peter Ward
Rachael Wardell
Guy Ware
Emma Warnock
Ellie Warren
Stephanie Wasek
Daniel Waterfield
Sarah Webb
Lucy Webster
Adam Welch
Clemency Wells
Nathan Wescott
Karl Ruben
   Weseth
Jo West-Moore
Mark Wharton
Tom Whatmore
Wendy Whidden
Robert White
Indra Wignall
Kyra Wilder
Claire Willerton
G Williams
Sam Williams
Sharon Williams
Courtney
   Williamson
Sarah Wiltshire
Kyle Winkler
Bianca Winter
Lucie Winter
Sheena Winter
Simon Winter
Astrid Maria
   Wissenburg
Stephen Witkowski
Jonathan Wood
Nathan Wood
Paul Woodgate
Emma Woolerton
Christine Wyse
Ben Yeoh
Ian Young
Juliano Zaffino
Sylvie Zannier
Rupert Ziziros
Carsten
   Zwaaneveld